Thad Planted a Kiss on Lyle's Lips.

"Oh, what a sweet mass of contradictions you turned out to be, Lyle Camden," Thad whispered, lifting his mouth from her own to nuzzle her throat, still warm and damp from the shower.

A shudder ran through her as she pushed against his chest, conscious of the accelerated beat of his heart under her hand. Or was it her own?

DIXIE BROWNING
grew up on Hatteras Island—her family has been associated with this region since 1739. She is an accomplished professional artist but thoroughly enjoys her second career—writing.

Dear Reader:

Silhouette Romances is an exciting new publishing venture. We will be presenting the very finest writers of contemporary romantic fiction as well as outstanding new talent in this field. It is our hope that our stories, our heroes and our heroines will give you, the reader, all you want from romantic fiction.

Also, *you* play an important part in our future plans for Silhouette Romances. We welcome any suggestions or comments on our books and I invite you to write to us at the address below.

So, enjoy this book and all the wonderful romances from Silhouette. They're for *you!*

Karen Solem
Editor-in-Chief
Silhouette Books
P.O. Box 769
New York, N.Y. 10019

DIXIE BROWNING
Tumbled Wall

Silhouette Romance

Published by Silhouette Books New York

America's Publisher of Contemporary Romance

SILHOUETTE BOOKS, a Simon & Schuster Division of
GULF & WESTERN CORPORATION
1230 Avenue of the Americas, New York, N.Y 10020

ISBN: 0-671-57038-2

First Silhouette printing October, 1980

10 9 8 7 6 5 4 3 2 1

America's Publisher of Contemporary Romance

Printed in the U.S.A.

Tumbled
Wall

Chapter One

Considering her perfectly natural fear of speed, Lyle had made pretty good time. She slowed down as she approached Oregon Inlet Bridge to admire her first glimpse of Hatteras Island. It had been a long time coming; even knowing her mother's all-but-forgotten connection with the Outer Banks, Lyle was not prepared for the quick surge of emotion that almost swamped her.

Had she made a mistake? The question hammered at her as she floored the accelerator of the aged Volkswagen to push it over the high center of the bridge. Ever since she was a child, shuttled from boarding school to summer camp to whatever other accommodations her renowned parents had decreed for their only offspring, she had been fascinated by the link with this far-flung barrier island.

She had subscribed to the biweekly paper that covered the area, pouring over photos and pouncing on any mention of the family Durant. Her mother had been a Durant. In fact, her professional name was still . . .

Oh, Lord! Even now it seemed impossible! She had seen little enough of her parents over the years. A gauche, ugly duckling who was nearing twenty-one didn't fit in with either the image or the life-style of two of the country's most popular, most beautiful duo-pianists. And then, in the one brief get-together they had had in ages, everything had ended in a spectacular car crash.

Lyle had awakened after almost a week in the hospital alone except for one new friend. It had been Stan Merrill who had gotten her through the months of recuperation and the hollow grief. However, she had never been in any doubt as to his motives, although he made a play of being fond of her for her own sake. A free-lance journalist who had only recently met the famous team of Camden and Durant, as well as their redheaded, freckled daughter, could have but one motive for courting her so assiduously.

She was used to it, of course; the disbelieving laughter, the ridicule—and worse. She had learned very early not to reveal the identity of her parents after being accused of either bragging or lying. She had hidden behind a wall of reserve and schooled her impulsive, redheaded nature to an unnatural rectitude.

Even now, when she was escaping at last to begin a new life, she was being less than honest about who she was and why she wanted this particular job. The name, Lyle Camden, had not meant a thing to Hestoria Durant. But if Lyle could convince her employer that she was suitably settled and mature, quite capable of finding contentment as a typist-companion in a house-hold of two old women, then she would have the secret

satisfaction of being with a distant relative—surely
there was *some* connection. Family, as such, held no
happy connotations for someone rejected by her parents as she had been, but still she could not bring
herself to cast off this possible tie. Surely it could do no
harm to warm herself on the edges of belonging.

She buttoned up the neck of the gray cardigan.
Making a clean sweep with her past, she had given her
best friend, Carol, all her fashionable, expensive
clothes, her jeans and boots and anything that might
raise suspicion as to why someone who was young and
could obviously afford the best, would content herself
working for a pittance for an old woman in a quiet,
off-the-beaten-track place like Frisco. Besides, since
the wreck, nothing fit her, anyway. She had lost weight
she could ill afford to lose during her month in the
hospital. Carol, oddly enough, had insisted that the loss
brought out a new beauty, hollowing out her cheeks to
reveal exquisite bone structure, but Lyle had listened to
the careless—and sometimes deliberate—comments
about her plainness for too many years to be taken in by
that.

She felt a growing sense of excitement as she
followed the narrow highway down the sandy stretch
between Pamlico Sound and the Atlantic Ocean. A tiny
smile brightened her expression as she thought again
of the ridiculous salary she had been offered; evidently Hestoria Durant was living in the past. Still,
her own skills were not that marketable. She'd probably earn just about what she was worth, given adequate room and board. It was ironic that after making a tremendous splash across three continents for
all these years, Reade and Julia should leave nothing behind. It had taken all their fabulous salary,

and then some, just to live up to the image they projected.

It was almost dark when Lyle turned off onto the sandy trail. There were no lights, no houses—nothing but reaching branches that scraped the sides of her car.

She leaned forward, peering through the gloom. Live oaks and loblollies, with gray beards of moss trailing down, seemed to take on sinister characteristics. It was isolated, all right! The first house on the road, her employer had written . . .

Heaven, was that it?

Weathered wood, funny little pointed shingles in tall gables, broken gingerbread trim and a complete absence of any welcoming beam of light, Durant's Knob stood facing her squarely, as if daring her to come any closer.

Lyle switched off the engine but left the headlights gleaming palely across the sparsely grassed sand. It had never occurred to her she might arrive to find the place empty. Somehow, from the letters they had exchanged, she had imagined that Hestoria Durant and her housekeeper were recluses.

Well, there was nothing to be gained from sitting here. Before she gave up and began looking for a motel, however, she might as well take a closer look. It was possible that they lived in the back of the house, for it was quite large for two women. They could have let darkness slip up on them without remembering to turn on the front lights. It was also possible they had not received Lyle's letter telling them when she would arrive. If only they had had a telephone, this might not have happened.

Once away from the influence of her car's headlights, Lyle was heartened to see a dim square of yellow streaming across the backyard. Churning through the deep sand she gave momentary thanks that there didn't seem to be a watchdog. Poking around a strange yard after dark could be hazardous. Still, what alternative had she? She had driven nine hours in one day and the thought of being turned away now that she had reached her destination was almost more than she could bear.

"Hold it right there!"

The distinct male voice came from behind her and Lyle swung around, her heart taking one enormous leap to lodge somewhere in the region of her throat.

"Who are you and what the hell are you doing here?"

She could see nothing except a large dark figure looming against the headlights and in her terrified state, the very trees seemed to take a threatening step closer, pinning her against the darkness.

"Is—is this Durant's Knob?" she choked when her voice finally found its way past the lump in her throat.

"It's Durant's Knob, all right, but what—?" Then, with a note of disbelief, "Pam? It's Pamela, isn't it? What on earth did you do to yourself, anyway? Hesty was expecting you last week, you young scamp."

"Pamela?" Lyle repeated the name weakly, feeling as if she had stumbled into the middle of a Hitchcock film where everybody knew the script except she.

A hand reached out and grabbed her chin, angling her face toward the light. "What happened to your hair? Last time I saw you it was flopping around in two mud-colored pigtails. Don't tell me you, of all people, finally sampled the hairdresser's art!" There was open amusement now, and it had the effect of lighting the fuse to Lyle's temper.

"I—you—let me go, darn you!" She struck futilely at the hand that clamped her chin.

"Hey, simmer down, honey! It's me, remember? Your old sparring partner! It's been five or six years, hasn't it? That can make a few changes," his eyes dropped the length of Lyle's body, "although there've been few in some areas, at that. Did you think I wouldn't recognize the scallywag who let all the air out of my tires and put the jellyfish in my bathtub?" He laughed wickedly, pushing a fist gently against the chin he still held. "You haven't lost the fire in your eyes, though, nor that stubborn little Durant chin, and once you wash that mess out of your hair, you might look half human again."

Lyle stood frozen with anger. Somewhere a dog barked and another, more distant, took up the cry.

"I—don't know who you are, or who you think I am," she managed through stiff lips, "but I've never seen you before in—my life and I—and I—"

The hand came up again. This time it lifted her chin only briefly before moving on to the hair Lyle had coiled so carefully that morning in her effort to look the part of a "settled, mature woman."

"No, it's not just the color, is it? Those mud-colored pigtails felt like limp rayon fringe, but this stuff—" His fingers twisted in her hair and Lyle winced. "This stuff is alive, aggressively alive! Just who are you and what are you doing here?"

Breathlessly, partly from anger and partly from some other emotion that might be fear—and might be something less easily definable—Lyle answered him. "I'm Lyle Camden. I was hired by Hestoria Durant as a typist and companion."

"I bet you were!"

"What do you mean? Of course I am! Why should you doubt my word?"

"I'll tell you why I doubt your word, little trespasser. Hestoria is eighty-one years old and she can't see worth a damn. All right, she's determined to write up the history of her family, despite the fact that there's no one left who gives a damn about it. The stock ran to seed a couple of generations back, except for Hesty, and the only bud on the family tree is Pamela, who, incidentally, will be more than enough in the way of a companion for her great-aunt, when and if she ever shows up! So even if you're on the level, Miss Comdon, I wouldn't unpack yet. You just might find yourself redundant."

"Camden," Lyle corrected tersely. "I still don't see what business it is of yours. If Miss Durant tells me to go, I'll go. Until then, I'll thank you to keep your hands and your advice to yourself!" Her chin was lifted belligerently, her face flaming, and she was making a valiant effort to steady a trembling lip. If she could not handle this first setback, she'd stand a poor chance of making a go at any sort of a future for herself.

The man made a mocking bow. "Thaddeus Creed, Miss Camden, not Comdon. If you're determined to stay, I suppose I'll have to let you in. Hesty and Ethel will be back in the morning. They had an ophthalmologist appointment in Elizabeth City. I'm the nearest neighbor and since we've had a rash of trespassers and a spot or two of vandalism lately, I'm just keeping an eye out."

That explained his suspicions, but it certainly didn't excuse his rudeness. Reluctantly, Lyle started to follow him but he stopped her. "If you value your battery, you'd better turn off your lights. I'll go in the back way and let you in the front."

"Is—isn't there anyone here at all?"

"Worried about the proprieties?"

She couldn't see his face but his tone was extremely offensive. "Don't be silly! I simply meant—well, maybe I'd better go to a motel and come back tomorrow." Her adrenalin-fed bravado was seeping away, leaving her achingly weary and slightly shaky.

"No need. The island's overrun with drunk fishermen and you'd probably luck out and run into one." He strode away without another glance.

Once inside the front door, Lyle looked around her curiously. It was old, not especially well kept, and the hall, itself, was bleak and unwelcoming, empty except for a golden oak monstrosity that bore with resignation an assortment of raincoats, umbrellas and scarves. The two windows, innocent of draperies, rattled their wavy glass as a burst of wind struck the side of the house.

"Your bags," announced Thaddeus Creed, dropping her suitcases beside her. Under the glare of the overhead fixture, Lyle took in his rather intimidating stature with a quick glance from under thick dark lashes. The uncompromising nose looked as if it might have been broken some time in the past and his jawline discouraged any attempt she might have felt to assert herself. The man seemed to be constructed of well tanned leather stretched over granite, the only softness being a thatch of dark, sun-streaked hair. There was certainly nothing soft about the hazel eyes that glinted with a metallic sheen.

As if aware of the scrutiny, he turned to stare directly at her and Lyle was unable to tear her gaze away from his rough, weathered features. "Seen enough?" His voice was as hard and rough as his appearance.

"Well, after all," Lyle excused herself defensively, "I really don't know anything about you. You might be a burglar, for all I know!"

"In which case you've put yourself in a pretty awkward position, haven't you? Come on," he continued impatiently, "I'll show you to a room."

She temporized; "I'll just—ah—rest on a couch somewhere."

"Oh, for heaven's sake, come on!" He seemed suddenly to have tired of baiting her. "You're in absolutely no danger from me—or any other man, I daresay."

There was nothing Lyle could say to that. Accustomed as she was to a lack of masculine attention, she was nevertheless stung by his open derision.

Hours later, as she lay in bed, Lyle wondered at the chain of events that had landed her here in a strange house without the knowledge of the owner. All her life she had struggled to subdue a quick, impulsive nature by forcing it to hide behind a reserved manner. If it hadn't been for the aggressive boorishness of that man, she'd no doubt have found a room in a motel instead of practically breaking and entering. As it was, she'd probably be out of a job before she'd even begun.

Pressed down by a quilt that must have weighed twenty pounds, Lyle considered getting up and sneaking out, leaving the island for good. Surely she could find something to do, somewhere!

No, damn it! Redheaded impulsiveness had gotten her into this fix and if she yielded to it, where would it end? As embarrassing as it was, she was determined to stick it out, if only long enough to meet her employer, who was probably a distant cousin.

If Lyle had been inclined to take seriously Thaddeus Creed's words about her possible redundancy, she was soon relieved of any worry. No sooner did Hestoria Durant shed her rusty black coat and hat than she shepherded Lyle into what she euphemistically termed the library to commence work.

Lyle had greeted her with a red-faced apology for having trespassed on her hospitality, only to be hushed in no uncertain terms. "Sensible thing to do, with me not here to meet you. Good thing Thad came along to let you in."

"Well, I'm so glad you aren't angry with me, Miss Durant. I honestly didn't know what to do. It was getting dark and I was so tired and Mr. Creed said—"

"Call me Hesty and let's get to work."

By the end of the first week, Lyle was on more or less familiar terms with the steadily decreasing branches of the Durant family tree. The fact that she found herself to be almost certainly a twig on one of those branches was a source of both joy and embarrassment to her.

She worried briefly about the so-called Durant chin as she underwent a fierce scrutiny from Hesty's faded brown eyes, but she had been spared by their inefficiency.

Having learned that first day that Ethel tolerated no interference with what she termed her bounden duty, which included cooking excellent meals and making halfhearted attempts to clean away the house moss, her term for the rolls of lint, Lyle settled into a regular schedule. Most of her time was spent sorting through old newspapers accumulated over the years while she also listened to Hesty's slightly acerbic accounts of the long- and shortcomings of her relatives.

During that first week Lyle was surprised to find Thaddeus Creed a frequent visitor. He dropped in unexpectedly and there was no tactful way she could avoid him. She tried to shield herself behind a wall of reserve, though she wasn't that certain she even wanted to avoid him.

Under Hesty's rheumy eye, he seemed to delight in baiting her, sprawling there like some indolent lion. Lyle parried his shafts effectively for the first few minutes, but he never rested until he had sent the color flaming to her face. If words wouldn't do it, then he simply looked at her, his piercing eyes ridiculing her old-fashioned clothes until she wondered if she had not gone a bit too far in her efforts to look older. Too late now, though—unfortunately.

What was she thinking of? As if it mattered what he thought of her! Well, all right, so he was—what was the word Carol used? Machismo? Sexy, she supposed it meant. He was that, all right, not that she, herself, was attracted to that sort of blatant masculinity. Yet whenever he succeeded in destroying her equilibrium to the point she was forced to flee the room, her face rivaling in color her flaming hair, she comforted herself with that thought.

One unseasonably warm day, Lyle washed her hair in the early afternoon and sought a sunny, sheltered place in which to dry it. She took the faded cotton blanket Ethel had offered her and spread it over the sand at the edge of the woods, and as the sun dried the coppery strands of hair, sending them into violent convolutions, she found her eyelids growing heavier and heavier.

Basking in the warmth of a late autumn sun, she rolled over onto her stomach, hiked her skirt up over her thighs and surrendered to sleep.

Something disturbed her. A tickling on her thigh, as if an ant or a fly had walked across her skin, sent her hand waving around blindly to brush it away. Her eyes remained closed and she nestled deeper into the warm sand.

For an indeterminate time she remained unmolested; then the tickling came again. Rolling halfway over, blinking sleepily up through the curtain of hair, she swatted irritably and caught her breath as her hand encountered something warm and solid.

In one swift, awkward movement, Lyle sat up, tugging her skirt down over her knees. "What are you doing here?" she demanded.

"Trying to decide whether or not I could light my pipe on your hair," Thaddeus replied mockingly.

Her senses drugged with sleep and sunshine, Lyle stared at the man who squatted before her, a dried seedhead in his hand. Before she could marshall her defenses he asked her if she were settling in.

"Yes," she conceded, suspicious of his bland inoffensiveness. Instinctively, she drew herself up into a small bundle, arms wrapped around her knees protectively.

"D'you like it here?" he asked.

"The island or the job?"

"Both, I suppose."

"Yes to both, then. Why?" She peered at him doubtfully.

Thaddeus shrugged and Lyle looked quickly away from well developed muscles that moved smoothly beneath faded flannel. "Looks as if I was wrong, doesn't it?" he asked after a moment's silence.

"Wrong?"

"About your being redundant. Seems Pam can't make it for awhile."

"She's not coming?"

"Oh, she'll be here in her own sweet time, but right now she's crewing on a sailboat headed for the Bahamas."

"Hesty didn't tell me," Lyle said.

"She didn't know until a few minutes ago. I have the nearest phone and Pam asked me to deliver the message."

"Oh," Lyle murmured. As usual, she felt uncomfortable in his presence, as if his very masculinity were a threat to her. She moved further away, and it didn't help matters when, peering sidelong at him, she caught the gleam of amusement in his eye. He knew very well how he affected her and he was doing it deliberately! Her mouth opened to tell him she preferred her own company when he forestalled her by blandly inquiring how the memoirs were going.

"They're not memoirs," she was quick to correct. "It's a family history, an *old* family, and I think it will prove an invaluable contribution, whether you think so or not!"

"Don't go all defensive on me," Thad protested mildly. "I've nothing against the *ancien régime*, it's just that I've always wondered how *new* families come into being. Maybe they burst full blown upon the earth, complete with a full complement of cousins, maiden aunts and shiftless in-laws. Think so?"

An irrepressible burst of mirth erupted from Lyle, to

her own surprise, and she met Thad's suspiciously bland countenance before turning quickly away. The man was either extremely droll or he was having a quiet laugh at her expense.

"As a matter of interest, Miss Camden, an invaluable contribution to what?"

"To—well, to sociology, to anthropology—history, maybe. Oh, what difference does it make? I can't guarantee it but I'll bet a hundred years from now someone might be darned glad Hesty took the time and trouble to collect and collate all that material and pass it on in coherent form."

Again that sardonic twist that passed for a smile. "I beg your pardon, Miss Camden. If I seemed to be making light of your work, it was only because I didn't understand the profundity of its nature."

"Oh, don't be so—so—"

"Superior?"

"I was going to say insufferable."

"I can no more help the one than the other," he grinned, and Lyle found herself unable, once more, to repress an answering grin.

Taking advantage of a momentary relaxation of the tension between them, Thad proceeded to entertain her with a highly colorful account of the island's history. He sat on the sand beside her blanket, his long, powerful legs drawn up and clasped in the same manner as Lyle's own, and told her about the way in which the earliest settlers in Jamestown had used the strand of islands as natural corrals, sending down men with their families to tend the cattle, and of the shipwrecks that had sent more than one half-drowned seaman ashore from the "Graveyard of the Atlantic."

"But what about the lost colonists? That was before Jamestown, wasn't it?" Lyle asked him, totally unaware of the way in which her eyes traced his features as he spoke.

"Yes, it was the first English colony here, and the first child born of English parents in the new world was born right there on Roanoke Island. There were Spanish-speaking people further south, of course, and the Vikings had left their calling cards in the form of an odd coin or two and some carvings in the midwest, but the fact that this eventually became an English colony and later, an English-speaking nation, gives more importance, I suppose, to the little group of people who came over here in 1586."

Lyle's eyes followed the movement of Thad's well-shaped hand as it sifted sand onto the edge of her blanket. From there it was but the blink of an eye to the muscular thigh so close to her own and she felt an unaccountable weakness in her limbs. She came to her senses to hear Thad saying, "So, since the only Indians who remained friendly to them were the Croatans, or the Hattorask Indians, who lived on the nearby island of Croatan, and the colonists actually carved the word, Croatan in one place and CRO in another, a signal they had agreed on if, for any reason they had to leave, it seems only logical to me that they went where they said they were going."

"But where *is* Croatan?"

"You might be sitting on it. Actually, it hasn't appeared on any recent maps, not in, say, about four hundred years or so, give or take a few. The inlets have changed all out of recognition since then, of course, but it seems Croatan was composed of the lower part of Hatteras and the upper part of Ocracoke."

"But if you knew where they went, why were they called 'lost'?" Lyle persisted.

Playfully, Thad tickled her under her chin with the

seedhead he still held in his hand. "Because no one ever saw them again, and, incidentally, while I might be able to give you a few years, I'm not quite old enough to have played a personal part in the affair."

"Yes, but didn't anyone ever look for them?" Lyle was determined to keep the conversation on an impersonal level.

"They didn't exactly send out an all-points bulletin, but Governor White, when he got back after being delayed by the Spanish Armada, found only remnants of their little fort and a few scattered personal possessions, the Indians and the elements had accounted for the rest, I suppose. He saw the messages they had carved, but for one reason or another, he didn't head for Croatan. Instead, he hightailed it for England and gave them up for lost—including his daughter and grandchild."

Another parent, another rejection—four hundred years apart, Lyle was thinking bitterly.

Thad continued, "As far as anyone knows, John Lawson was the next person to visit Croatan, or Hatteras as it was becoming known. He reported auburn-haired Indians with blue and gray eyes who, as he put it, 'valued themselves greatly for their affinity to the English,' and said some of their ancestors could talk from a book. But that was a hundred years later, so who knows what really happened?"

Lyle was as fascinated by Thad's soft island accent as by his words, although it was much less concentrated than Hesty's Elizabethan cockney brogue.

"I don't suppose it really matters," Thad concluded, "but living down here for Lord knows how many generations, you get sort of caught up in the mystery of it all." He turned suddenly to catch her eyes on him and for a long moment they stared at each other, neither of them speaking. Then cool, impersonal shutters dropped down over his eyes, wiping out the warmth of the past few minutes, and Lyle was chilled. It was as if he had deliberately withdrawn the tenuous hand of friendship he had extended, having thought better of it for some reason of his own.

He stood and brushed the sand from his close-fitting jeans. "Well, Miss Camden, I guess I've bent your ear all out of shape. You'll have to accept part of the blame, though, if I've rattled on and bored you with a dull lecture." The familiar mockery was strong in his eyes.

"It wasn't dull," Lyle protested wistfully.

Her attitude only seemed to provoke him. "Quite the little listener, aren't you? You must have read in one of those women's magazines how to get your hooks into a man. If you can't get what you want with your *beaux yeux*, you can always fall back on being a good listener—if you're short of other—ah, attributes, that is."

Wild color flooded Lyle's face as she scrambled to her feet, ignoring the hand Thad extended. "And just what do you think I'm interested in getting from you, Thaddeus Creed? I don't know what sort of women you're used to, but they must be pretty dreadful specimens! But then, what other type would even look at someone like . . ." Her voice dwindled away as she stared at his hard, uneven features. He could not by any stretch of the imagination be called handsome and yet there was something so arresting about his looks, so blatantly sexual, that Lyle stepped back, shaken by her own thoughts.

"Don't be shy, Miss Camden. I haven't frightened

any children lately, but I'm under no illusions about being just another pretty face. That makes two of us, doesn't it?"

Lyle stared at him, her face drained of color until it was parchment pale, each freckle standing out in relief. Her hands twisted nervously and her eyes held a curiously vulnerable look, as if she were hearing the echoes of taunts that had hounded her throughout her life.

Perhaps it was that very look of vulnerability that caused Thad to mutter a soft expletive.

Lyle yanked up the blanket and turned away, stumbling slightly in the soft sand. The skirt of her navy blue dress flapped limply about her calves and her hair was a wild, red cloud about her head. Just before she reached the back door, she slowed. She had warmed so readily to the earlier friendliness Thad had shown, been fascinated by the stories he told her. Was it to come to nothing because of her quick defensiveness? Perhaps he hadn't meant to be insulting. Perhaps if she apologized for her hasty words . . .

"Mr. Creed, I'm sorry if I—well, I had no right to make personal comments about—well, about your— women," she broke off, helplessly confused. He was not going to help her out at all and it was at least as much his fault as her own. Stung by her own embarrassment, she blurted out, "Nobody with an ounce of sensitivity would have said what you did about my—my *beaux yeaux* and my—doubtful attributes! I can't help my looks!"

"But then I never claimed to have the least bit of sensitivity, Miss Camden," he replied with infuriating calmness. "And as to the sort of women I'm accustomed to, that's my business, isn't it? Or are you looking for a few vicarious thrills to brighten up that drab little life of yours? And as for not being able to help your own looks, you puzzle me, Miss Camden. Indeed you do. If I were a suspicious sort, I'd say you were a lot younger than you pretend to be."

Poised warily, Lyle stared at him while the late afternoon sun made a nimbus of her hair and touched off a strange luminosity in her dark blue eyes. "You can just go to hell, Mr. Creed," she finally managed in a strangled tone before whirling about to run for the security of the house.

Chapter Two

As the days began to grow shorter, Lyle spent hours rearranging and cleaning books, a chore she found useful for times when Hesty's eyes bothered her. She had discovered early that her employer did not tolerate pampering.

"Postcard from that traipsin' young'un," Ethel announced one afternoon as Lyle struggled through a newspaper account that supposedly concerned either a Durant or an in-law.

Hesty was dozing in her chair, a habit she stoutly denied. "Well, bring it here, bring it here!"

"I'm a-comin', jest let me get outten me raincoat," the housekeeper grumbled from the hall.

"Here, Miss, reckon that'll set ye up right smart."

Hesty squinted at the colorful card and handed it over to Lyle; "Here, read it to me, girl. The child never could write a proper hand."

" 'Back in the states. Had a ball! See you as soon as I change my duds. Love, Pam.' "

"Humph! Believe it when I see it," Hesty snorted.

"Thad said she hadn't been here in six years," Lyle ventured, curious about the girl ever since Thad had mistaken her for Pamela that first night.

"Oh, she's been here, all right. It's Thad ain't been here. Fool boy was off to the mainland too long!" In Hesty's estimation, no sensible person would spend any more time away from the island than was absolutely necessary. "First it was all that schooling, then some fancy job or another, but he finally took sense and come on home where he belongs. Might have happened sooner but for that Darnette girl."

Ethel had returned to the kitchen and Hesty leaned back in her chair, closing her eyes for an instant. Almost immediately she snapped them open again to glare at Lyle accusingly. "Dust gets in 'em, that's all," she grumbled. "What was I saying? Oh, yes, that gal of Thad's. Well, she's a looker, I'll not deny her that, but she didn't do right by the boy. Folks always thought they'd make a match of it, but she took some notion about wanting to live away from here and next thing we knowed, she'd upped and married some feller from Currituck County and Thad, he come back home and never said word one! Humph! Fool girl!" She set the rocker into motion with a heel, toe tapping against the varnished floor. "Thad was worth ten times the other feller with all his money and fancy yachts!"

Not caring to hear any more details of Thad's love life, Lyle changed the subject. "I wonder when Pam'll get here."

"Oh, she'll turn up before long, if only to remind me she's a-waiting for this old house of mine when I ain't got no more use for it." Hesty cackled. "Child ain't no fool, for all her raising. Knows danged well she's the last of the Durants and makes no bones about wantin' this place when I'm gone to my Maker. Like her gumption, I do! Speaks her piece!"

Silence reigned for awhile, broken only by the protesting creaks as the old house stood against the northeast wind. After awhile Hesty began to speak again, recalling Durants who were only faded names on yellowed paper to Lyle: Redheaded Putnam who had a fight with Papa and ran off to sea, never to return again. Lyle's thoughts blocked out the thin old voice as she resisted an impulse to touch her own flaming coil of hair. She had somehow thought that all the Durants were dark, like Hesty.

The drone continued, telling about Nobel, who was too proud to wear his glasses and nearly ended up marrying the wrong sister by mistake, about Montgomery, who had literary pretensions and who always wanted to be called Monty, but who was known as Gummy all his life.

Again Lyle's own thoughts drifted off, recalling bits and pieces of family history she had picked up as a child, before Reade and Julia struck it rich by parlaying a guest appearance into a TV series of their own. Julia's father had gone to sea as a young man, for a Wilmington ship owner. Later, he married the owner's daughter and they had one child, Julia, who was born after her father was lost at sea in a tanker collision. Julia had been brought up by her mother's family in Wilmington and had inherited both her mother's beauty and her musical ability, the latter to such an extent she had won admittance to Juilliard, where she met and married Reade Camden.

Bitterness crept into Lyle's thoughts as she finished the story from personal knowledge; Reade and Julia Camden, like George P. Durant and his wife, Emma, had had one child, a daughter, but the gods had turned their backs, for neither the beauty nor the musical ability had carried to the present generation. They had been disappointed in their only offspring, a fact neither of them had been skilled at hiding, for she had grown too tall, too skinny, all but tone-deaf and painfully shy as a result of her shortcomings. The final irony, could they but know it, was that their daughter now found herself back at the starting point, the ancestral home, as a paid employee.

Having made a conscious effort to avoid Thad Creed since the day he had found her drying her hair, Lyle was disgusted at her own lack of self-discipline in giving in to her curiosity. She had heard Hesty speak several times of Thad's home, no more than a few hundred yards further along the trail, and today, taking advantage of one more warm, sunny afternoon, she found herself walking east along the Great Ridge Road. There were only the two homes in the immediate area and when she came in sight of an unexpectedly modern house, she leaned against a gnarled hornbeam to study it.

Instead of the modest cottage she had expected, she saw a large, imaginatively designed construction of redwood and glass, its abstract form blending surprisingly well with the surrounding natural woods. Unthinkingly attempting to see through the gray-tinted glass, she was startled to hear something crashing through the brush only yards away. She ducked beneath a hanging vine in time to see a small deer bounding away through the tall marsh that Hesty called the sedge.

Poor thing! She must have practically stumbled over

it. Looking quickly for the best way through the tangled growth, she edged along a low hummock, hopping over low shrubs, twisting her way through briars and trailing vines to get another glimpse. Just as she was ready to give up, she spotted it standing motionless on another knoll, staring back at her. Oh, it was beautiful! Graceful, gentle . . . she sidled out further, ignoring her damp shoes as they sunk deeper and deeper into the muck.

"Here, darling," she called softly. How did one call a deer? She took another step and lurched as one foot slid on the muddy bank, grabbed a handful of vines and barely managed to retain her balance. The swamp was deceptive; it didn't *look* that wet. Regretfully, she watched her quarry bound out of sight, then glanced down at her feet.

"Yuk!" Really, in this kind of country, jeans and boots were the only thing. Anyway, she was beginning to think her own idea of what an older, settled woman would wear was a bit "little theater," but it was too late now.

"Are you crazy?" Thad roared from not five feet away.

She whipped around, entangling herself in a catclaw briar that seemed determined to hang her.

"Don't move, you imbecile!"

"Don't yell at me!" she yelled back, moving and causing the briars to dig in with a vengeance.

Hopelessly caught, she could only wait. He was beside her in three swift strides, lifting the vines from her hair, her shoulders, her skirt. Ducking from beneath a trailing tentacle, she leaned away from him, hating his closeness, leery of the patience and gentleness he was exercizing in freeing her from the mess she had landed in.

"Watch it—you'll tear—hmmm," he muttered, carefully removing a briar from her skirt. "There, I think that does it." With that he lifted her beneath the arms and began retracing his steps to the trail.

"What do you think you're doing? Put me down!"

"Behave yourself, you stupid woman! Stop it before I drop you!" He lowered her in the clearing and reached up to untwist a twig from her hair. "Now, will you stop sputtering and tell me what you were doing here spying on my home?"

"Spying! Why you—you insufferable pig!" she squealed, her temper in no way improved by the painful scratches that were beginning to make themselves felt all over her body.

"There's not much to see here *except* my house, so if you were all that curious, why didn't you just march up to the front door and demand the guided tour? Or do you just naturally prefer sneaking around backyards?"

"Oh, shut up! For your information, I was following a deer!"

"All the way from the Knob?" he jeered.

"No, not all the way from the Knob! I was—I was taking a walk and I heard something in the bushes!" she cried.

"And hearing something in the bushes, you naturally waded into the swamp after it without a second thought. Oh, you're real bright, Lyle Camden, you really are! How have you managed to survive all these years?"

"Well, I'm certainly not afraid of a deer, if that's what you're insinuating, and I'm reasonably sure there aren't any bears or alligators here. What should I be afraid of except maybe big, blustering bullies like you?"

"Big blustering bullies, hmmm. Alliterative, if slightly dated, my dear lady." He was openly amused now and his mocking sneer lighted Lyle's fuse.

"Why do you always treat me as if I weren't quite bright or something—as if I were up to no good?"

"Up to no good!" He pounced on that one. "Oh, that's even better! Next you'll be calling me a bounder, an unregenerate cad. Just for the record, Lyle, where have you been all your life?"

Curled up alone with a stack of books, she might have answered; there was safety between the covers of a romantic novel. "I guess I ought to thank you for untangling me," she said ungraciously, ignoring his question.

"Save it until I've finished with you." He took her arm and propelled her toward his house.

"Wait a minute," Lyle protested, pulling away. "I can't go in there, I'm muddy."

"My place is closer than the Knob and there's a little matter of poison ivy that needs to be tended to before it's too late."

"Poison ivy! Don't be ridiculous, in November?" she crowed.

"In November or any other month, given the dose you've inflicted on yourself."

"But those were just briars!"

"The ones that dug in were. The rest were good old Rhus Radicans, almost as virulent in its dormant stage as it is green. The worse case I've ever seen was contracted in December and you, with your thin skin, ought to be highly susceptible. Now, will you quit shying away and come on? A good scrubbing might prevent the worst of it."

They were almost at Thad's front door by now and it was childish, she supposed, to resist his efforts to help her. He couldn't help his naturally abrasive manner, she decided charitably.

One quick glance at his rugged face as he ushered her through the door and all her doubts returned; there was something distinctly cat and canaryish about the gleam in his eye.

She could not suppress a gasp of admiration as they entered. A crude boor he may be, but he lived in an understated elegance that must have cost a fortune! Surely those were genuine Tabriz and Cabistans on the gleaming floors.

"You approve?" he asked mockingly.

"It's stunning." Regardless of what she thought of the man, she could not hide her spontaneous appreciation and just for a moment a strange expression flickered across his face. It was gone almost instantly, to be replaced by the familiar sardonic coolness. He put a hand at her back and urged her forward. "Come on, then, let's tackle your scrubbing up."

Kneeling before her, he slipped off her shoes, then frowned up at her. "What about these things—tights or whatever? They look ruined to me. Better climb out of them so I can get to those scratches. You've still got a few spurs in you and they'll get infected unless we get rid of them."

Flustered, Lyle frowned down at her pantyhose. "Where can I take them off?"

"Matter of fact, it's going to take more than just a quick once-over with a damp cloth to do the job.

Shower would be best, I guess. There's no telling where you've been exposed, face, hands, legs, come on, I'll show you."

Uncertainly, she stood up. This whole situation was getting out of hand. "Look, I'd better go home," she said doubtfully. "A few more minutes won't make any difference, surely."

"A few minutes can make the difference between a minor rash and a mass of weeping blisters that can become infected and give you more grief than you bargained for. You need to get out of those clothes as soon as possible, they're contaminated with sap."

Thoroughly alarmed now, Lyle followed. She was hardly aware of the large, beautifully furnished bedroom as he crossed to open a door to the adjoining bath.

"Everything you need, I think. I'll get a bar of laundry soap. Might be a little harsh," he said, frowning at her tissue-like complexion, "but it's better than the alternative. Scrub down with that, then finish up with toilet soap if you want to. I'll get you something to put on."

"I can wear my own things," she protested quickly.

"Don't be silly. Just be a good girl and do as I say, hmm?" He turned away and was back within a few minutes to find her standing where he had left her. "Get a move on, Lyle, or do you need some help?" Again the quick, mocking glance. He dropped a thick terry cloth robe on the bed and handed her a bar of yellow soap and as she glared at him defensively, he winked and left the room.

Using a loofah, Lyle scrubbed herself from top to bottom until she was certain she had removed several layers of skin. She blotted one leg and looked down at it apprehensively. The angry red skin was marked with a variety of scratches and at the rate it was beginning to sting, she was not sure the cure wasn't worse than the disease!

Shrugging into the robe he had provided, she wondered again how she had managed to embroil herself in such a ridiculous situation.

"Aren't you through yet?" Thad called through the door. "I offered to help, you know."

Irritably, Lyle glared at the closed door, then took her time straightening the bathroom before stepping out into the coolness of the adjoining bedroom. Uncertainly, she stared around her at the understated color and the satiny paneling.

"Like it?" He spoke from behind her and Lyle spun around to see her host lounging against the bathroom door.

"How did you get in here?" she demanded.

"The bathroom has another door, you know," he grinned wickedly. "I'm surprised you didn't bolt it."

"I didn't even notice it," she glowered, acutely uncomfortable to find herself alone in a bedroom with this man, wearing nothing except his own bathrobe. "All right, I'm scrubbed raw. May I please go home now?"

"You act as if I were threatening your virtue instead of rendering first aid."

"Don't be silly! I want to go home!" she exclaimed.

"Nobody's stopping you," he shrugged. He moved closer, with an expression on his face that Lyle profoundly mistrusted, and she took a step backward to come up against a dresser.

"Poor Lyle. Poor little maiden lady. I wonder if you're blushing at your own imagination or if you've just taken off one too many layers of skin." He reached out a hand and touched her cheek and Lyle shied away, her eyes wide with apprehension.

"D—don't be ridiculous! It's only that my—my skin is so thin. I—I scrubbed too hard and—stop that!" she cried, now thoroughly alarmed as Thad, with one deft touch, sent her hair tumbling about her shoulders.

He leaned back, hands on his lean hips, head to one side, and studied the results of his action. "It's beautiful! Why the hell do you screw it up like that? I'm absolutely amazed, Lyle Camden, at how debauched you can look, you with your prim mannerisms and your missionary barrel clothes. Who are you trying to fool, Lyle, and more to the point, why?"

"I'm not trying to fool anyone," she snapped, and because she was stunned with the ease with which she could lie, she blushed furiously, compounding the effects of the vigorous scrubbing.

Thad threw back his head and laughed and as Lyle darted past, intent on escaping, he grabbed her sleeve, pulling the robe from her shoulder.

Short of leaving the thing behind, there was nothing she could do but halt her flight and this she did, spinning around to face him with her mouth opened on a furious tirade.

The tirade was silenced before it even began as Thad's mouth came down on hers with a kiss that sent her reeling. It bore no resemblance to Stan's rather tepid advances and as the seconds passed, she was horrified to find herself responding with an ardor she never knew she possessed. Aghast, she renewed her struggles to escape.

"Oh, what a sweet mass of contradictions you turned out to be Lyle Camden," Thad whispered, lifting his mouth from her own to nuzzle her throat, still warm and damp from the shower.

A shudder ran through her as she pushed against his chest, conscious of the accelerated beat of his heart under her hand. Or was it her own?

"Stop that," she gasped between clenched teeth, hating the exquisite thrills that coursed down her body as his teeth made tiny little nips along her neck. "You—you beast!"

"Ah, yes," he murmured quizzically, loosening his hold so that she managed to push him away. "The maiden lady bit. How about, unhand me, you brute!" He laughed and his hands dropped from her shoulders.

Lyle, finding herself suddenly free, felt unaccountably chilled and for long seconds she just stood there, her eyes shimmering at him through unshed tears of anger, hurt and embarrassment—as well as something that felt suspiciously like disappointment.

It was far into the night before sleep finally came. The memory of her reaction to Thad's attack—what else could it be called?—frightened her and even as she struggled to understand her own feelings for the man she hated, she sensed something else, some elusive emotion that darted away before she could recognize it.

The worst of it was, he had kissed her as some sort of a joke, she thought despairingly. Some perverse streak of malicious humor seemed to find great satisfaction in baiting her whenever they met, and today had been the final humiliation.

He had bundled her own clothes into a paper bag, dropping her shoes in on top of them with a comment about her ridiculously small feet, and when she protested that she couldn't walk home barefooted, he had reached out and grabbed the knotted belt of the robe she still wore and pulled her close to him.

"What's the matter, little Lyle, don't you trust me to get you home safely? You're carrying on like the old maid you pretend to be, or rather like the adolescent I half suspect you are. One of these days, Lyle Camden, I'm going to unravel you and see what you're all about."

Lyle was trapped against the hard warmth of his body, her senses filled with the scent of him, the sight and the feel of him and she could hear the sound of her own pulses beating against her ears.

"One for the road, hmm? Payment for services rendered?" Thad growled, capturing her lips again with no trouble at all.

Lyle was helpless as his mouth parted her own lips. He moved his head slowly, working his mouth against her own until her legs threatened to collapse. Whatever this wild power was that transmitted itself from his body to hers, nothing in Lyle's life before had prepared her for it. As his hands rounded her hips to press her even closer, she whimpered against his lips, like the mewing of a helpless kitten.

"Had enough, Miss Camden?" he murmured huskily, grinning down into her face as if it were all a huge joke.

A joke. That's exactly what it was to him! She was used to taunts, used to laughter about the ugly duckling who came from a pair of swans, but no one had ever dared to go to such lengths before, and it hurt! It hurt worse than anything she could have imagined.

Perhaps something of her bewildered misery reached him, for Thad eased her away from him, running his hands up to her shoulders and squeezing before releasing her.

"Don't try to figure it all out, Lyle, honey. A man's a peculiar beast subject to all sorts of whims when he finds a pretty girl in his clutches."

"Don't laugh at me, Thad Creed," she whispered, "and don't call me pretty when we both know I'm not."

"Does it bother you? There are all sorts of beauty, you know, and prettiness is the least of them. Now come on and I'll take you out to the car and get you home. Tell Ethel to throw in an extra handful of detergent when she washes out your things and from now on, stay out of the bushes, hmmm?"

Chapter Three

Perhaps if several days had elapsed before Lyle had seen Thad again, her embarrassment would have grown all out of proportion but he came around just after lunch the next day, seeking her out in the library.

"Any sign of a rash?" Not a gleam marred the perfect gravity of his face as he continued, "You look a bit pinker than usual but that's probably the soap. Harsh, but still the most effective preventive I know."

"I'm fine, thank you," she replied stiffly. "The scratches will heal in a day or so and I'll be as good as new."

"Just as if it had never happened, right? No permanent damage." He *was* teasing! That mocking glint flickered in and out as he tried vainly to subdue it!

Lyle bridled, then forced herself to cool down. It would never do to rise to his bait. "No permanent damage whatsoever, thank you," she assured him calmly, turning back to her task.

"Good! Now, how about taking a day off to help me with Hesty's Christmas shopping?"

Her eyes flew up to see if he was serious. "Why do you need anyone to help you?" she asked cautiously.

"Well, it's not easy for a man. She insists on getting something for every member of her old Sunday School class as well as half the congregation, and it usually falls to me to do the shopping."

"Well, if you're used to it, you certainly don't need my help," she told him witheringly.

"Hesty suggested it," he told her blandly. "You see, I've always had—ah, feminine assistance, but this year I'm on my own."

"Why don't you get whoever usually helps you to do it?"

"Not available," he shrugged, looking resigned. "Oh, well, I was afraid after yesterday you wouldn't want to help me. To help Hesty, that is. You, uh, wouldn't have any idea of what to get for females between the ages of, say, fifty and ninety, would you? I can probably think of something for the men but the women's gifts always defeat me." He dropped down into Hesty's lopsided rocking chair, hands hanging loosely between his knees. "Peanut brittle—that's a good old-fashioned candy. Mustache wax, maybe, and whiskey, of course."

Lyle giggled in spite of herslef. "Oh, all right, I'll come with you, but I'm doing it for Hesty's sake, understand that!"

"Well, of course you are, so am I," he assured her. He gave her such a palpably false look of indignation that Lyle's lips trembled, then they both burst into laughter.

"Tomorrow morning about nine suit you? Hesty said she'd be entertaining a delegation from the church and

I expect both she and Ethel will be too busy to do anything else. The epic will have to wait."

"Maybe I'd better harvest a little house moss from the front room before company comes. Ethel believes in letting it grow," Lyle said, wryly amused. She was slightly dazed at finding herself on such relaxed terms with Thad Creed. He had the most disconcerting way of catching her off-balance, no matter what she expected of him. She pulled the remnants of her dignity about her and announced coolly that she needed to get back to her job, if he didn't mind, before Hesty came down for their regular afternoon session.

"How's it going? Making any headway?"

"Mostly reminiscing, so far. That's important, too, of course, because Hesty wants to use as much personal information about everybody as she can, but—well, I feel like such a fraud. I mean, I'd expected to have a manuscript to copy when I applied for the job, but so far, I've mostly just listened." She looked at him anxiously. "We do get a good bit done, though, considering all these newspapers and things that had to be gone through. Most of them were almost too brittle to handle, and to make matters worse, Hesty can seldom remember just why she saved them. I have to go through every page looking for a familiar name."

"You don't have to defend yourself to me, Lyle. I'll admit I thought it was a pretty silly idea in the beginning. I was afraid Hesty's eyes would give out on her completely, but I can see now that you actually save them for her. Without you, she'd still be trying to do the job and we both know she's not up to it."

"Just as long as you don't expect us to come up with a finished book anytime soon."

"I told you you don't have to defend yourself to me.

The most important thing, as I see it, is making Hes happy. She can't get out anymore, she can barely see to read, and let's face it, her friends are no more able to visit her than she is them. As for family . . ." He shrugged and Lyle felt her face grow warm. Oddly enough, she had almost forgotten the secret of her own relationship, so well did she fit into the household. It seemed that, acknowledged or not, ties were tied before one ever realized it. So much for her treaty of noninvolvement.

Thad was studying her from beneath lazily narrowed lids. "As I said, the most important thing is to keep her happy, to keep her mind occupied. I guess having a fresh audience gives her a new lease on life. I think I mentioned once that you were a good listener, didn't I?"

Seeing that sardonic smile, Lyle felt something shift in the region of her heart and she busied herself with her papers, sliding several of them on the floor in her nervousness.

Thad carefully gathered them up, handed them back to her and told her he'd collect her in the morning.

The sun shone brightly but it was not enough to warm the gale force winds that swept across the low-lying islands. The heavy car whipped along the narrow strand, rocked occasionally by a ferocious burst of wind and Lyle nestled into the warm, luxurious interior, acutely aware of the man beside her. He smelled of a clean, mossy fragrance combined with wool and tobacco and the sight of those powerful hands easily controlling all that horsepower brought an odd weakness to her midriff.

They shopped together, selecting scarves, woolen

gloves, tobacco and mufflers as well as a variety of sweets, not including peanut brittle. Thad suggested a break for lunch and hurried her into a seafood restaurant where they both agreed the clam chowder was almost as good as Ethel's.

Over fried trout they discussed the plastic paneling and furniture to be found in so many commercial establishments and from there they went on to talk of the exquisite woodwork in Thad's home. "Labor costs being what they are today, putting up paneling board by board is prohibitive, out of the question in some cases. I was able to justify it in my own home, of course, because it's more or less a showplace."

Lyle thought that was a bit conceited of him, even granting that the place was exceptionally fine. Noticing her skeptically lifted eyebrow, Thad grinned and set her straight.

"I'm an architect, after all, and it's my own design. If I chose to bypass the shortcuts, surely it's only good business. It's the sort of home I'd rather build, but of course, on big commercial jobs, one uses a different method altogether."

Nonplussed, Lyle could only stare at him. "Do you know, I never really thought about what you did for a living. Not that there's any reason why I should, of course, but—well, most of the men I've seen since I've been living at Frisco seem to go and come without any semblance of a schedule. Nothing nine-to-five, I mean."

"Oh, there's a schedule, all right," he told her, his eyes crinkling attractively. "If you'll excuse me for bending a cliché out of shape, fish and tide wait for no man. In these parts, though, the men tend to be a pretty independent lot and most of them can claim several occupations."

"At least that explains why you live all alone in that big place. You do, don't you?" She wished she could swallow the embarrassing question she had just asked. It was none of her business and just because they were all warm and well fed and relaxed was no reason to drop all her guards. Thad Creed was just the sort of man to take advantage of any lessening of her defenses.

"I do, except for a five-carat diamond named Bertha-lee Willis. She can work circles around any other five women and her cooking's cordon bleu, Outer Banks variety. Trouble is, she's gone almost as much as she's there."

"What happens when she's gone?"

"When she's there, it's very, very good and when she's gone, it's horrid."

"To bend another cliché," Lyle gurgled.

They left the steamy restaurant and Lyle pulled her collar up around her neck, wondering if she dared invest in a pair of boots. She thought longingly of the soft rust suede ones she had given Carol, considering them unsuitable for the conservative, middle-aged woman Hesty had specified in her advertisement.

How ironic to think that a short while ago she had bought whatever she needed in the way of clothing, never worrying about the cost. When one's parents were outrageously highly paid television stars, one expected to be able to dress well as a matter of course. While Lyle's tastes had never been particularly flamboyant, running more to simple styles and subdued colors, she had appreciated quality and it had been quite a bad shock to find herself all but penniless.

"Hmm?" She glanced up to catch the look of amusement on Thad's face.

"Where were you? I said, if you like, we'll run into that pottery place I told you about, then head for home. Nothing else we need for Hesty, is there? What about you? Need anything?"

Dismissing the boots from her mind, Lyle stretched her legs to reach his long-legged stride and agreed to drop off their parcels before going on to the pottery shop. They had almost reached the car when someone spoke behind them.

"Thad! Is it? Oh, darling, it is!"

They both spun around at once and Lyle's eyes widened at the sight of the exquisite creature standing—posing, really, she thought with a flash of uncharitableness—with both hands outstretched.

"Cora! What on earth are you doing here?" Thad exclaimed, turning toward her with a smile that lighted his whole face.

"Oh, darling, you're just the man I wanted to see. Have you had lunch? You *must* take time to advise me, Thad, please," she wheedled prettily.

Feeling totally superfluous, Lyle stood where she was and watched as the woman pulled Thad's face down and kissed him thoroughly. Only the fact that he was loaded down with parcels kept him from returning her embrace, Lyle thought sourly, turning away to put her own things in the back of Thad's car. She hesitated for a moment, wondering if he planned to introduce her, but Cora Whatshername was talking a mile a minute and Lyle was freezing.

Climbing into the front seat, she huddled disconsolately into her upturned collar, seeing again that kiss and, in spite of herself, comparing it to the one Thad

had given her the other day. Then he had been playing a malicious prank, teasing her because he knew exactly what she was feeling, trapped, to all intents and purposes, in the bedroom with him. There was nothing even faintly teasing about the kiss he had just given his friend, Cora, but then, there was quite a difference between the petite, mink-clad woman, whose beautiful face looked like porcelain enamel, and the great, gawking redhead with a flaming face and a bathrobe six sizes too large!

The low-lying sun shafted a beam through the windshield and Lyle sneezed. Just as she fumbled for a tissue, the door opened and Thad leaned in to speak. "Lyle, I want you to meet Cora Lambert. Cora, this is Lyle Camden."

Lyle leaned down awkwardly to look up at the other woman, murmuring a how-do-you-do as she clutched the tissue and tried to suppress another sneeze.

To no avail. The sneeze erupted and Thad turned back to Cora. "I'd better get this child back to Hesty before she catches cold. I'll give you a call and we'll get together, all right?"

"I'll be staying at the cottage, darling, at least for a few more days before I go back to Elizabeth City. Who knows when I'll be able to use the cottage again." A shrug of her shoulders and an attractive little moue prompted Thad to take her hands in his. He had disposed of his packages by now and that left him free to kiss her good-bye, Lyle thought, disgruntled as she valiantly resisted the temptation to look out the back window.

During the trip home, Lyle seethed with questions she had absolutely no right to ask. Thad was obviously sunk in his own thoughts, for he barely managed more than a dozen words before pulling up in front of the Knob.

"Here, I'll help you in with this pile. Looks as if you'll be stuck with the chore of wrapping them all."

"It's no chore. I don't mind in the least," she retorted, thoroughly out of sorts for no good reason.

"Don't tell me you're one of those people who goes all soft and soggy over candycanes and tinsel angels," he teased.

Lifting her chin unconsciously, Lyle replied coolly, "One doesn't have to get all soggy, as you put it, to enjoy the holiday season."

He laughed outright and tapped her on the nose. "What a complex, funny little creature you are, Lyle Camden. One of these days . . ." He left it at that and Lyle, staring at the door that had closed behind him, wondered if the ache she felt had anything at all to do with Thad Creed and Cora Lambert.

Pamela Durant arrived and Lyle forgot all about Cora Lambert. If she did not forget about Thad Creed, it was not for want of trying, for she was only too aware that her self-imposed rule of noninvolvement was being seriously threatened by the man who, in spite of all she could do, was infiltrating her defenses.

Without being aware of it, Lyle had built up a preconceived image of Pamela Durant and the girl who strolled through the door, backpack on her shoulders, was a complete surprise. Instead of a browned, carefree young woman with a sexy, sunbleached mane of hair swinging to her shoulders, she was a thin, short-haired girl in slightly rumpled khaki shorts and crew-necked pullover, wearing hiking boots and knee-length socks.

"Pamela?" she asked cautiously, pausing on her way to the library with two cups of coffee.

"Who the heck are you?" The girl demanded, dropping her pack unceremoniously and stretching her arms above her head. "Wow, am I aching! Hitched a ride on a Honda 350. Never again! Got another cup of that stuff? Oh, and how about a sandwich or something? I'm starved!"

More amused than annoyed, Lyle murmured something about taking Hesty her coffee, to which the girl replied that she'd take it, not to bother.

"She's in the library," Lyle told her, handing over the steaming mug.

"Well, la-de-da! The library, no less. Last time I was here it was the junk room." Pamela took the coffee and marched off with it, calling out to her great-aunt as she went.

Shrugging, Lyle took a sip of her coffee and returned to the kitchen to fill Pamela's order. It had already struck her that, dressed as she was in her gray denim shirtwaist with the blue smock she often wore over it to work, she might easily have been mistaken for a domestic. For that matter, who was she to quibble over the relative positions of a domestic worker and a typist-companion? An employee was an employee— and a Durant was a Durant, she finished wryly.

"Lyle's been a-helping me with the family history," Hesty explained after introducing the two girls minutes later. Her eyes, squinting against their own deficiencies, moved back and forth between them. "You two gals could almost be the same age," she speculated. "Be nice for Lyle to have somebody young in the house. She's had nobody at all to talk to 'cept Thad."

"Good heavens, Hesty, put your specs on!" Pam retorted sharply. She eyed Lyle curiously, ending with an expressive snort, and Lyle, partly amused, partly irritated, arose to take the coffee things out. As she left them she heard Pam, who didn't bother to lower her voice, exclaim, "Where on earth did you find her, Hes? Don't tell me Ethel's finally packed it in."

Lyle didn't wait for Hesty's reply. She cleared the tray and handed Ethel the coffee mugs.

"Done riled ye already, has she? She'll speak her bit, that one, but leastwise, you know where you stand with her."

As Ethel sat down at the table, Lyle took over the dishes, a minor triumph in itself. Ethel, whenever the wind was from the northeast, bringing on a worsening of her "rheumatics," now allowed Lyle to wash dishes and even to help with the preparation of the food, if not with the actual cooking.

Before she finished the dishes, Lyle remembered that the room she had used since her first night at the Knob was the one set aside for Pamela. After a survey of the others, it had seemed the only course, since, despite its size, the house boasted only five bedrooms, one of which was filled with the accumulation of decades and the other, smaller one, was so damp and cold it was all but uninhabitable. According to Ethel, it leaked and was, consequently, badly mildewed.

It took no more than fifteen minutes to affect the changeover and to remake Pamela's room with fresh linen. She finished the job just before the other girl came upstairs, fortunately, for she had no desire for any girlish chitchat, nor, she was certain, did Pamela. While she might have gotten away with her charade as far as Hesty and Ethel were concerned, Pam was another matter. She wouldn't miss much and Lyle could ill afford to have her asking awkward questions about age and background and why someone like Lyle should chose to come to such a small place to work at such a dull job for such a tiny salary.

When Hesty went upstairs for her rest after lunch, Pam dashed up after her and was down again within minutes, having changed into a long, lavender cotton dress and a black sweater, worn with her same boots. She met Ethel in the hallway and as they exchanged a few words, Lyle had a chance to study the girl unobserved. Her features were quite good, her jawline was lean and graceful, ending in a small, cleft chin. Her nose, small and straight and her brown eyes large and expressive. Her skin was sallow, true, and her hair lank, but her figure, while lean to the point of thinness, was graceful enough.

Suddenly Lyle caught her breath. That chin—Lyle's own chin. What was it Thad had called it? The stubborn Durant chin? And the other features—oh, oh! She could only hope no one would look beyond the differences in coloring, for she and her cousin were too much alike for comfort.

"Thad still here?" Pam was asking Ethel, then, not even waiting for an answer, "I'll run over and see him. It's been years! Is he still the macho hunk he used to be or has old age set in?"

"Go 'long, Pam, you ought not to talk like that."

"Ahh, Eth, times have changed since you courted your country boy in the schoolyard playground after supper."

"Pamela Durant, you hush that mess!"

Pamela just laughed and, tossing her shawl about her shoulders, announced that she would probably be out all afternoon. "Guess I'll go by and see the Burruses. I reckon old Zeb's married by now, but Johnny'll never settle down."

"You know Zeb ain't married, nor likely to be, missy. You can't fool me none."

It was after dark when Pam got home again and she dropped down into a chair, legs sprawled out before her, and lighted a cigarette. "Damn, Thad has to go to Elizabeth City tomorrow, wouldn't you just know it! The day after I get here, too!"

Hesty, dozing in her chair, opened one eye and grunted. It was all the response Pam needed, evidently, for she continued in the same disgruntled vein. "It's that Darnette woman, I'll bet anything. I thought he'd finished with her when she ran off and got married, but now that she's back in circulation, she's got him on the hook again, I hear. Old witch! She been down here yet?"

Hesty emitted a gentle snore and Pam turned to Lyle for an answer. Lyle shrugged and said she hadn't met anyone of that name that she recalled.

"Oh, she married—what was his name? Some fellow from Currituck who made a fat bundle by turning his farm into a fancy hunting lodge. That was before she married him, of course. Now she's left him—or he's left her. Either way, it's bad news, because poor old Thad's always been a sucker for her and no doubt she'll figure he's worth marrying now that he's made it as an architect, even if he wouldn't move away from here. She always hated the island. Lambert, that was his name. The man Cora Darnette married, I mean."

"Pamela, if you don't mind, I think I'll go upstairs. I really don't know anything about the matter, anyway."

"What's the matter, too good to gossip?"

"No, not at all. I just make it a policy not to discuss things I know nothing about." Even to her own ears that sounded unbearably smug, but it might serve to cut off talk that was getting uncomfortably personal.

"Oh, holy saints! Just what we need to liven up the old place, a goody-two-shoes! Well, if you won't lower yourself to the level of us common folk, how about a rousing game of dominoes before cocoa and beddy-bye?"

In spite of herself, Lyle grinned, and Pam, catching it, responded in kind. "Yeah, well—sorry. One thing I've never been accused of is being a nice person. And while I'm groveling, sorry about shoving you into the dungeon, too. Better you than me, though."

"The dungeon? Oh, the bedroom. That's all right. I knew you had dibs on the other one when I came but I didn't see any point in changing before I had to."

"Right. Well, if it rains, shove your bed away from the wall and you'll be all right."

The next few days followed the pattern established by Lyle and Hesty earlier, with a short working session in the morning, a break for lunch, after which Hesty rested and Lyle, exercizing a good bit of tact, helped Ethel with the housework. On fine days, she went on a walking exploration of Frisco, occasionally venturing as far as the ocean, although even on the sunniest days, the wind that whipped in off the pounding surf soon penetrated her warmest clothes. But she carefully avoided walking in the direction of Thad's house, even when she knew he was not at home.

There was usually another work period later on in the afternoon and then, after dinner, Hesty would recall anecdotes she wished included in the life and times of the family Durant, often wandering off on tangents, sometimes dozing in the middle of a story.

It was an easy schedule, one Lyle felt almost guilty about, calling as it did, for so little effort on her part, but Hesty declared herself well satisfied.

Of Pamela she saw little, for she seemed to have something planned for every day, usually something that included the two Burrus brothers. Zeb, the oldest, was a quiet, weathered man in his late twenties who treated Pam much as he would a tagalong child. His sober but somehow attractive face would crinkle indulgently as he waited for her to clatter down the stairs, while Johnny, the younger of the two brothers, would tease Hesty and Ethel unmercifully, bringing a sparkle to their faded eyes with his wickedly handsome smile. He treated Lyle with a charming irreverence from the first and she was quick to notice the dark looks from Pam whenever he teased a little too familiarly. No one ever suggested, though, that Lyle accompany them when they went out.

The weather, with one of those sudden changes so typical of the Banks, turned wet and ferocious and Ethel took to her bed with a heating pad and a bottle of liniment. Hesty was fretful and not inclined to work, which suited Lyle just as well, for she had her hands full with Ethel's chores. She wondered how the two of them managed before she came, but then this winter they were both a year older. Perhaps last year had been easier on them.

The rain came down in horizontal sheets and Lyle's bedroom stayed miserably damp, taking on a mustiness that threatened to be permanent. Lyle would not admit, even to herself, that she missed Thad. As far as she knew, he hadn't returned from Elizabeth City and she couldn't help but wonder if his staying had anything to do with Cora Lambert. The thought was distinctly unwelcome. From the fragments she had heard from Pam, Hesty and Ethel, she had learned that Cora Lambert, née Darnette, had been the inspiration for the house Thad had built. Not by one word had he revealed his feelings when she married someone else; according to Pam, he had simply completed the house and moved in, as if that had been his plan all along.

Illogically, the thought of someone so arrogant and seemingly invincible as Thaddeus Creed being humiliated by any woman made Lyle hurt for him. She was not at all certain she even liked the man, despite the fact that he disturbed her senses more than she was ready to admit. All the same, she knew too well how rejection could hurt and she wouldn't wish that pain on her worst enemy. To lead with your heart and then find you'd been made a fool of—oh, no, not for someone like Thad Creed. This curious ambivalence she felt toward the man was confusing, but she knew she didn't wish him that humiliation.

Chapter Four

"Boy, you look like death warmed over," Pam greeted Lyle over breakfast.

"Thanks," Lyle mumbled, dropping into an empty chair. The rain had continued through the night and despite her best efforts, Lyle had not been able to avoid the leaks. She had awakened cold and shivering to find half her bed soaked, her eyes burning and her head stuffed full of cotton. By the time she dressed and came downstairs, the stuffy head had turned into a three alarm headache.

"Bad night, huh," Pam murmured sympathetically. "I told you to move your bed over. If it keeps up much longer, we'll all be afloat. As soon as it slacks I'm going up on that roof and patch the biggest leaks if I have to do it with umbrellas!"

"You're not, neither, Missy, and don't you let me hear you a-climbing up on that roof!" Ethel admonished loudly, causing Lyle to wince.

"Don't worry, I'll get some help. Zeb and Johnny owe me after all the elbow grease I've put in on those

56

boats of theirs." Hearing the kitchen door open, she turned and exclaimed, "Thad!"

Ignoring the newcomer—and hoping he, in turn, ignored her flaming face, Lyle got up to get herself some aspirin.

"How's it going, young'un? Miss me?"

"You know it, man! What's in Elizabeth City that you had to hotfoot it as soon as I got here? As if I didn't know!"

Shutters dropped down over steely eyes. "Getting a bit out of line, aren't you, Pam?"

"But Thad, she's not—"

"Any of your business," he finished smoothly, turning to look at Lyle. "Morning, Lyle. You don't look so great today."

"Thanks a lot," she retorted sarcastically. "Like death warmed over, according to Pam."

"Talks too much, doesn't she?" he observed easily, swatting Pam on the backside as she got up to get him some coffee.

Hesty and Ethel came in and Thad stood and seated Hesty as Ethel began whipping up more eggs.

"What you dosin' up for, Lyle?" Ethel demanded.

"Headache." She reached for a glass of water with which to wash down her pills only to have it removed from her grasp by Thad.

"Had any breakfast yet?" he asked, scrutinizing her pale features closely.

"I'm not really hungry," she muttered, reaching for the glass and frowning at him as he emptied it in the sink.

"Sit down and have some eggs first. Then if you still need it, you can have a pill," he instructed in an infuriating manner.

"Don't tell me what to do," Lyle bristled.

"Then don't act so foolish." He took her by the shoulders and pressed her down into an empty chair and before she could protest, he began working on the muscles at the base of her neck. "You're like granite," he said after kneading away for a minute. "Redheads are notoriously high-strung."

"Hair color has nothing to do with it, and anyway, it's my head that aches, not my neck," she grumbled, relaxing in spite of herself as his strong hands worked their magic. Her eyes closed and for a moment there were only the two of them.

"Boy, the hired help gets first-class treatment in this establishment. How about a job, Hes?" Pam said facetiously.

"Don't be fresh, girl," her great-aunt retorted.

"Here, Lyle, you eat this an' you'll not need no pill to set your head straight. Now, me legs is another matter. They gave me fits last night."

"Ethel, I'm not going to massage your legs, no matter what you say," Thad laughed, running his hands lightly down Lyle's arms as he stood back and took his seat.

The odd intimacy of a moment ago was gone, and surprisingly enough, so was her headache. Lyle was suddenly aware of a powerful sense of well-being as she looked around her at the four people seated around the formica table. How quickly they had become important to her, how insidiously easy it had been to slip into a comfortable niche in this household, a niche from which she would never want to be displaced. A moment later her illusion was shattered as Thad announced the imminent arrival of Pam's parents.

"Medwin? Why, he's not been here for Christmas

since, let's see—was it 19 and 67? That was the year Lorrie's twins both come down with the appendicitis and got wrote up in the Coastland Times. I come across it just the other day."

"Good Lord, what does *he* want?" Pam exclaimed.

"Likely the same thing you do, Missy, and don't call your pa *he.*"

"Well, the last thing I heard, *father* dear," she added an expressive emphasis, "and mother were off to Key West for the duration with old man Palmerton. I can't see 'em deciding to rough it here at the Knob unless he's suddenly got some bee in his britches."

"You can work out the whys and wherefores later," Thad told her. "In fact, you might even put it down to family feeling. Is it so hard to believe Medwin might actually want to see his aunt?"

Pam looked disgusted. "You know him as well as anybody. Can you honestly see him doing anything unless there was something in it for him?"

"You've become shockingly cynical, young lady. Maybe it's time you had your eyes opened."

"Huh! They've been open, that's the trouble."

"Never did learn no respect fer your elders," Ethel accused.

"I give them the respect they earn," Pam defended.

By this time, Lyle's head was beginning to ache again and she stood up quietly and got herself an aspirin, turning in time to see Thad's eye on her in what looked almost like sympathy. He shrugged helplessly and Lyle spared him a small smile.

"Well, all I got to say is, somebody better tell me where I'm a-gonna put 'em," Ethel declared, stomping across the kitchen to plunge her plate into the dishpan.

"Oh, heavens, that's right," Pam groaned.

"We'll make do, ne'er mind," Hesty soothed, but Lyle saw the furrows deepen on her forehead.

"I don't suppose you'd have them, Thad," Pam suggested slyly.

"Afraid I've already agreed to have some old family friends, the Simpsons. That about fills me up."

"Well, Lyle will just have to take her vacation. She'll have friends and family she'd rather spend Christmas with anyway, and that'll work out just right," Pam decided, talking across Lyle as if she were not even there. "When are they coming, Thad?"

"The twenty-second through the twenty-fifth."

"Hmm, Christmas day. O.K., Lyle, you can be off then," Pam declared, laying plans like a young general. "I can move into your room—boy, that's filial devotion for you—and ma and pa can bed down in my room. There, that's all settled. Now, Hesty," she turned to her great-aunt with the air of one who has taken the first jump and is approaching the second, "As soon as this rain lets up, I'm going to get Zeb and Johnny up on the roof to find those leaks. It's one thing to leak on Lyle, but quite another if I'm going to sleep in there." She smirked as if she were joking but Lyle was not so sure she was not serious. As Ethel had said, at least she spoke her mind, like it or not.

During the days that followed, Lyle thought with dread of the approaching holidays. Not even to herself would she admit how disappointed she was not to be included in the family plans. She couldn't remember the last really family style Christmas she had had—a cocktail party in San Francisco with a group of television people hardly counted—and to miss out on one that was sure to include Thad was too painful to contemplate.

Ah, stop wallowing, girl, she chided herself, attacking a pile of newspapers with renewed vigor. It's only a few days and then, when you come back, you'll be ready to start on the actual manuscript. She looked up as Pam came in, dressed in one of the two dresses she alternated with slacks and jeans.

"Ever been engaged, Lyle?" she asked, dropping into Hesty's chair and lighting a cigarette.

"Great scot, no," Lyle laughed.

"No, I didn't really think you had," she continued with unflattering frankness, adding, "I don't guess you've even had a boyfriend, have you?"

"No, not really. Why?"

"Oh, nothing," Pam shrugged. "D'you believe in marriage?"

Without hesitation, Lyle assured her that she did. After all, Reade and Julia had been perfectly happy with each other, even if they had been slightly less than ideal as parents. Unbidden, a picture of herself with Thad Creed formed in her mind and she made a deliberate effort to crush it.

"How about you? Anyone on the horizon?"

"You don't think I go for all that death do us part stuff, do you? Just a scheme for making lawyers rich, if you ask me. No, if I ever get interested in a man—that way, I mean, I'll live with him first. Then, *if* we still care for each other and *if* we decide to have children, then I might consider getting married."

"And what if the first one doesn't pan out and you try a second, and then, maybe a third," Lyle remarked sarcastically. "After all, it's easy, nothing to hold you together. Where does it end?"

"Ah, you sound like my mother. Charter member of the double-knit set, complete with weekly bridge luncheons, weekly hair appointments and weekly fights with Dad over money."

"It doesn't have to be that way, you know," Lyle told her quietly, not certain how she knew, just sure, somehow, that for a few lucky individuals, love was a reality and marriage the anchor that held their lives steady.

"Well, anyhow, I'll be too busy with my hostel for anything like that. Besides, these days, lots of people pass it up."

"What hostel?"

"Durant's Knob Hostel, what did you think? It's mine, you know. Hesty promised and she'll keep her promise because she knows if Dad gets his greedy little hands on it, he'll sell it within a week. Hesty s strong on family and she knows I'll hang onto it. I've got this plan, see, that'll make it pay for itself."

There followed a long description of Pam's plans for the Knob and, surprisingly enough, they sounded completely plausible to Lyle.

After supper the mood of friendliness persisted and Pam followed Lyle upstairs to her room. Cautious not to reveal her plans for Christmas—or her lack of them—to Pam, Lyle shifted the talk to clothes.

"I like that dress you had on yesterday," she said diffidently. It had been a lovely shade of violet but worn with a heavy black sweater, it lost its effectiveness.

"Oh, yeah. I sort of do, too. Zeb thinks it's stupid to wear long dresses all the time, at least he *says* he does, but I think it's neat. Romantic, you know?"

Swallowing her surprise, Lyle mentioned the boots Pam wore day in and day out.

"Oh, I have another pair, but these are so comfortable. Besides, they drive mother up a wall," she grinned. "What about those things you wear? Where'd you get 'em, P.T.A. Thrift shop?"

"Are they really that bad?" Lyle was chagrined, knowing full well they really were.

"You know, you're not all that bad looking, or at least, you wouldn't be if you did something about your clothes and hair. Do you have to wear it like that? It makes you look positively ancient."

"There's not a whole lot I can do with it, it curls so. At least this way, it's manageable. I don't have to have one of those dreadful weekly appointments," she teased.

"Touché. Anyway, I'm a nice one to talk. I've been thinking about doing something to mine, but I don't know . . ." Pam ran a hand over her short, utilitarian cut.

It really was mud-colored, Lyle thought, remembering Thad's description that first night. Nice though, warm, sunshiny mud.

"Why don't you spiff up a little over the holidays? Sort of a New Year's resolution. Who knows, it might make a difference," Pam said.

"A difference to what?" Lyle was amused at the direction the talk had taken, considering the way they both looked at that moment.

"Can't tell, you might even knock old Thad off his roost. It would save him from a fate worse than death, at least."

"I hope you don't mean that in the traditional sense."

"Not likely. I'm pretty crazy about him, though, and I hate to see him tangle with dear Cora again. She's on the prowl and the poor love is a pushover for her. If I didn't have other fish to fry, I might give it a whack myself. Hesty always planned for us to get together, did she tell you?"

"You and Thad?" Lyle asked, stunned.

"It's a hoot, isn't it? Not that he'd ever look at me, when all the girls on the island are nuts about him. He's so rugged looking. He's scrumptious—sexy, if you know what I mean."

Lyle was still attempting to come to terms with the idea of Pam and Thad. "Isn't he a little too old for you?" she asked tentatively.

"I'm eighteen and a half and he's oh, about thirty-four, I guess. Trouble is, I've known him too well since I was little. He'd never think of me as grown up. I probably wouldn't even have thought of it, myself, but Hesty has this thing about the last of the Creeds and the last of the Durants. Cora spoiled him for anybody else, though. Shame. I'll bet he'd make a terrific lover." She stood up and examined herself in the mirror before going out of the room. Lyle, lying back across the bed in relief was only glad Pam had not seen the wild color that had flooded her face. It might have been hard to explain.

The day before Lyle was to leave on her vacation, she had made up her mind to stay at a new motel at Nags Head. She had heard Thad mention it to Hesty, commenting on the design, and it seemed as good a place as any. It would be nice to stay right on the ocean, for as narrow as Hatteras Island was, it took time and energy to cut through the dense woods and trudge the mile of deep sand to the surf.

Late on the evening of the twenty-first, she carried her one suitcase out, leaving only her toilet case ror the morning. If she could get away as quickly as possible, there would be less time for awkward questions. She put the bag in the trunk and turned to see Thad approaching.

"Leaving tonight?" he greeted.

"No, just getting ready for an early start tomorrow."

He glanced derisively at the slightly battered-looking car. It bore small resemblance to his sleek Mercedes, but it had proved its worth on the trip to the island.

"Your right front tire looks worn. When's the last time you had them realigned?"

"I had them what?" she asked, puzzled.

"Good heavens girl, how long have you had a car, anyway?"

"I bought it to make the trip down here. Why?"

"You need a keeper," he replied witheringly.

Stung by his derision, Lyle slammed the trunk down and turned to flounce off. Really, as if everyone who bought a car automatically became a mechanical genius! Lyle, who was defeated by anything more complex than a can opener, had been quite proud of herself when she passed the driving test the first time out.

"Hold it," Thad ordered, grabbing her arm. "I'm not letting you take off who knows where in that piece of junk without having it checked out first. You go on inside, I'll be back after awhile."

"Where are you going?" she demanded, pulling her arm away.

"Just down to the service station. Where are the keys?"

"In the ignition, where do you think?" she retorted indignantly.

He groaned. "Where else, indeed? Remind me to tell you the facts of life sometime, will you?" He climbed in behind the wheel and Lyle was maliciously pleased to see how cramped he was in the small space. Serves him right, the big oaf!

When he got back, she was in the living room alone, having declined an invitation to accompany Hesty and Ethel to a special Christmas program at the church. It was a rare outing for Hesty and ordinarily, Lyle would have loved to go with her. She struggled to rationalize her staying behind, reluctant to admit that the only reason was that Thad would soon return.

He tossed the keys to her, leaned against the wall and reported tires, oil and fuel all right and the battery passable. "How far are you going?" he asked.

Lyle shrugged, scrambling wildly for an answer that would not lead to embarrassing questions. "Who knows? We may decide to visit several places. I'll be back late Christmas day, though."

"I wouldn't drive any further than you have to. Let someone else take their car if you plan to do much traveling."

"Oh, don't fuss so! How much do I owe you for gas and service?" She crossed to the table where her purse lay and the action brought her close to where Thad lounged. He reached out and pulled her against him.

She could have avoided it. His action was deliberate, unhurried, but there was nothing at all casual about the way he held her, his hands moving restlessly over her back as if striving to press her closer, until he was only a breath away. "I'll miss meeting you under the mistletoe, Lyle, so this will have to make up for lost opportunities." His lips touched hers, so softly at first that she wasn't sure it was happening, but then, with a stifled groan, he parted her lips and plundered their sweetness, driving away all rational thought and leaving her a bundle of pulsating nerve endings.

When at last he let her go, she almost fell. He stared at her, taking in her enormous, bruised-looking eyes, the swollen lips that still trembled from his assault, and the madly fluctuating color in her face.

"Lord," he breathed, "you have an unfortunate effect on me, Lyle Camden. If I were smart, I'd get the hell out of here while I still could."

"What do you mean?" she whispered, watching his eyes change from black coals to splinters of ice. The coldness that seemed to creep over his features like a sudden frost left her even more shaken than she already was.

"For a skinny, freckled redhead with abominable taste in clothes and absolutely no sophistication at all, you have a way of getting under my skin," he said in a clipped tone. "Maybe I've been holed up down here a little too long."

"Maybe you have, Mr. Creed," she returned stiffly. Her chin lifted and she picked up her purse and removed several bills. "Here, I hope this will cover what I owe you. You really shouldn't have bothered." She held out the money and he didn't move a muscle. Finally, she put it down on the table beside him and fled the room.

She rushed upstairs, hearing the front door slam behind her with a force that rattled the panes in the windows and Pam called out from the bathroom wanting to know what all the ruckus was about.

"Oh, nothing," Lyle temporized frantically, "I just forgot something and had to come back for it." She fell across her bed and wept silently.

Unseasonal it might have been, but Lyle was glad of the warm fog that hovered over the beach. It had taken her only two hours to reach her motel and she had immediately gone out to walk the shore, opalescent as the sun attempted to break through the fog. She spent most of the first two days walking alone, sometimes taking a sandwich out to eat in the shelter of the dunes. It was preferable to dining alone in a room filled with couples and family groups.

When the fog coalesced into a dispirited rain, she drove up and down the strand, stopping in first one place and then another. By Christmas Eve she had quite a collection of postcards and brochures. She did her best to avoid thinking of Thad, for she knew with a dread certainty that he spelled danger. He made no bones about the fact that he considered her ludicrous, a homely, badly dressed nobody without a vestige of sophistication. If he kissed her now and then, it was only some sort of cruel joke, a malicious response to the foolish infatuation she was unable to hide.

Unable to stand the empty beach, where thoughts impinged too freely on her consciousness, or the loneliness of her room, Lyle decided to search the shops for some token gifts to take back to the women at the Knob. She was struggling with the balky lock on her car door when someone hailed her and she spun around to face Stan Merrill.

His quick scrutiny resulted in a look of dismay across his regular features as he asked her what on earth she had done to herself. "What's with the tacky bit? You incognito or something?"

"Long story. Not a particularly newsworthy one, though."

He had the grace to look embarrassed and Lyle

hastened on to ask what he was doing in the area. It turned out he had been covering the First Flight Anniversary at Kitty Hawk and from there they proceeded to make plans for a day together. Lyle had no wish to be alone with him, so she insisted on spending the morning shopping. It was over lunch, with the booth beside them stacked with the small things for Hesty, Pam and Ethel, plus a large dress box for herself, that they were greeted by another familiar voice.

"Lyle? I thought I recognized that carrottop. I've forgotten the last name, I'm afraid," Cora Lambert cooed. Even as her eyes devoured Stan's conventionally handsome face, she asked if Thad were with her.

"No, he's not. This is Stanley Merrill, Mrs. Lambert. Stan, Cora Lambert."

She joined them, of course, and soon she and Stan were chattering about the First Flight celebration and several other noteworthy events in the area, leaving Lyle to her own thoughts. These thoughts were running in an altogether unacceptable direction when she heard Cora asking about the stack of parcels. "Christmas shopping?"

"All but the big one," Stan answered for her. "Found a dress that simply *was* Lyle and insisted that she have it. Can't have her running around like a refugee, considering who she—"

"If you're ready to leave, Stan, I'd like to have a few hours on the beach before dinner," Lyle interrupted repressively. She knew very well what he had been going to say and she leveled him with a look. He made it sound as if he had bought her the dress, instead of simply telling her how much it would become her. She had weakened to his blatant flattery and bought the damned thing and now she wished she had never seen it.

She spent Christmas Eve alone in her room with a paperback romance. Stan, she was quite certain, was at a party Cora had mentioned and she sincerely hoped she had seen the last of them both. At least Stan shouldn't bother her again, for there was nothing deader than yesterday's news—too late now for the "inside story."

The next day there was time for a long walk on the beach before check-out. The wind had blown the fog away and it was sparkling cold, exhilarating as the spume was blown all the way across to the dunes. Like a long, cold shower, it had the effect of clearing away the untidy emotional ends of her turbulent thoughts, leaving her free of her distaste for Stan, free of her demeaning jealousy of Cora and free of her fruitless longing for Thad.

The mood persisted as she topped Oregon Inlet Bridge and she caught her breath at the spectacle of the sun settling into a flaming reflection over the Pamlico Sound. She searched for a parking spot as she rolled off the bridge, intent on walking back out onto the fisherman's catwalks that lined each side of the bridge. Before she knew it, she had passed a perfect place and she glanced quickly behind her before whipping into a turnoff, around the median and back out onto the highway, giving only a cursory look to the right and left.

Later on she was almost certain there had been no car visible when she pulled back out onto the highway, but before she could even complete her turn there was a screaming of tearing metal, a screeching of tires and she was flung violently against her seatbelt.

Into a small silence that seemed hollowed out of the

noise, she became aware of a steady drip, drip, drip. Someone was yelling and then there was no time to think about anything as hands reached in to lift her carefully from the wreck.

"I seen it! I was coming after bait when this here lady come out o' that road and this here feller he come a-barreling around that curve like a bat outta hell!"

Lyle's head slowly ceased spinning and she looked around her carefully, still not sure she was in one piece. There were several fishermen and three men in Coast Guard uniforms and over the next thirty or forty mintues she was taken to the nearby Coast Guard Station where she was plied with over-sweetened coffee and asked countless questions. A sense of unreality was beginning to give way to an assortment of aches and pains and a nightmare feeling of *dèjá vu* when she heard a familiar voice.

"Come along now, Lyle, you can wait in my car while I clear up the details here."

Had she dredged him up out of pure longing? For a fanciful moment she wasn't sure. "Thad! How did you get here? How did you know?" she exclaimed shakily.

It seemed she had automatically given his name as having the nearest phone and she knew now there was no one in the world she wanted or needed more than this man who was ushering her calmly out to his car.

Chapter Five

Despite the warmth of the blanket he had spread over her Lyle could not stop trembling as she waited for him to finish with whatever needed doing back there. She stared unblinkingly ahead, seeing neither the dunes and beachgrass nor the big flock of snow geese circling low over the marshy soundside, but only the split second when her windshield had tilted and she had heard that horrible, familiar sound.

"Stop it!" He had returned and she had not even noticed. As he slipped into the seat beside her, Thad ordered her in a low, authoritative voice to snap out of it. "Think about something else—anything, but get your mind off what just happened. It's all over, no one was hurt. You're damned lucky to get out of it with no more than a hard shaking up."

"I know," she whimpered softly.

He started the car and they headed south. Even though she stared straight ahead, Lyle could sense the grimness that had settled over Thad's features. It came at her in great waves, as if he were controlling his anger only through the strongest effort.

"S—say something! Don't just—just freeze me like that," she pleaded, her voice barely audible over the purr of the engine.

"All right, I'll say something. Your car is a total write-off. I had it towed away and one of the Coast Guardsmen offered to buy it for parts. He has one of the same vintage. I told him you'd be in touch later."

"B—but how can it be a write-off? He only hit my fender, didn't he? It wasn't even wrinkled in front."

"Wrinkled? No, not this time, but evidently it had been wrecked before you bought it, Lyle. The whole frame is buckled. Besides, you have no business running around in a flimsy little car like that, knowing no more about them than you do."

"What do you mean? What difference does that make, and how am I supposed to get around, and—and—" Tears came, and once started, they flowed harder and faster as sobs wracked her body.

Without a word, Thad pulled the car onto a grassed strip of shoulder and switched off the engine. Roughly, he pulled her to him and pressed her head against his chest, holding her forcefully until she ceased to struggle.

Still she wept, unable to control the sobs that tore through her and after awhile, she became aware of the soft, tender murmurings against her hair and of the gentle hand that stroked her back. When she was quieter, he turned her deftly so that she lay almost in his lap, her wet face buried against his neck.

Gradually, the weeping subsided to an occasional sniffle and Lyle felt a handkerchief being pressed into her hand.

"Better now?" he asked.

"Hmmmhmmm. S—sorry to be such a baby," she apologized weakly.

"No apologies necessary," he assured her, his voice rumbling low from deep inside him.

Lyle peered up at him through the gathering gloom and saw quite clearly the tiny wrinkles that fanned out from his eyes, the deeply etched lines that bracketed his mouth and the proud thrust of his arrogant nose.

"How did you find out?" she asked him, more composed by now.

"Deputy radioed. I got the call just as I was leaving the house, fortunately. A minute later and I'd have missed it. I burned a track in the highway getting here, young lady, so if I collect a ticket for speeding, I'll hand it over, hmm?"

"You do that," she laughed shakily. "I owe you that much and more. Thanks, Thad. I—I don't know what I would have done without you."

She raised her face to him, all too conscious of how she must look. Tears had never come easy to her and Lyle knew she was not a woman who cried beautifully. He was only inches away and as she gazed deeply into his eyes, anxious that he should know the full depth of her gratitude, she said, "I owe you for this, Thad. If there's ever anything I can do for you . . ." she left it hanging. What would a man like Thad Creed need from someone like Lyle Camden?

He resettled her and started the engine. They were nearly at the turnoff before Thad spoke again. He seemed almost hesitant and when he pulled off the road and turned toward her, Lyle was aware of a strange feeling of uncertainty radiating from him.

"What is it? Why are we stopping here?"

"Lyle, I hate to have to tell you but Hesty had a heart attack yesterday." He hurried on, speaking over her horrified exclamations, "It's not a particularly serious one, if any attack could be termed not serious. Particularly at her age."

"But I didn't even know she had a heart condition," Lyle protested, her own troubles forgotten.

"None of us did, except maybe Ethel. Hesty's a wily old bird and she's kept it under her hat, but it turns out that this is not the first time. I wasn't here the last time it happened or I'd have known about it."

"But why did she keep it a secret?"

He shrugged. "Who knows? Pride, I suppose. Probably didn't want to give Medwin any excuse to put her in a nursing home."

"But he wouldn't—he couldn't if she didn't want to go, could he? Why should he be anxious to have her move out? It's not as if he wanted the place for himself. Pam told me she—"

"Pam? Oh, don't worry, I know all about Pam's plans for the hostel. Not a bad idea, really, It tickles Hesty to hear her go on about it. I think she admires Pam's spunk and outspokenness."

"They're a lot alike, aren't they?" It struck Lyle for the first time that this was true.

"Yes, as far as character is concerned, Pam's got her matched, but physically, she's more like her cousin."

"Her cousin?" Puzzled, Lyle shuffled mentally through the carefully compiled lists and could come up with no answer.

"Don't you think it's about time to end the charade, Lyle?" Thad spoke matter-of-factly and Lyle caught her breath as his meaning sunk in.

"How did you know?"

"Something clicked, then everything fell into place. I'm amazed that you thought you could get away with it."

"But how—?"

"Remember how I mistook you for Pam the first time I ever saw you? It was too dark to see your hair color clearly and with no clues as to coloring, you're remarkably alike. Dark blue eyes could be dark brown ones in the half light, your hair is no darker or lighter than Pam's, even the dusting of freckles didn't show up then. All I saw was that high, round forehead, those cheekbones, that straight little nose, slightly elevated, if I remember correctly, and that chin, that was the clincher. Stubborn as all get out, with cupid's cleft in the center. Then I got all tangled up in that wild, red hair of yours and forgot everything else."

"But when did—everything fall into place?" she whispered, "When did you know who I was?"

"Hesty's great-niece or Camden and Durant's daughter—the long lost granddaughter of G. Putnam Durant?"

"Then you know everything," she sighed, drained of all but a sort of empty relief that at last, she could be herself again, for what it was worth, no more pretending.

"I'm not such a cultural goose egg. I've been to a few concerts, even watched a little television. What I am is dense not to have caught on right away, given the name, Camden. Out of context, it just didn't strike me, even knowing all Hesty's tales."

"Then you know about—last July? They're both—"

"I know, honey. Try not to think about it just now, if you can help it. You're here now, and as Hesty's relative, you've got another problem on your hands.

Medwin and Pauline left last night. Pauline's hopeless—hysterical. Medwin, poor old man, is not much better. How Pamela rose above a pair like that amazes me. Well, at any rate, we've got to get organized, as they say in the movies. Pam's bedside manner is not one of her strong points, but between them, she and Ethel can cope with all but the nursing. I've put in for a nurse as soon as one can be found, but no telling when that'll be. Looks as if you're elected. Think you're up to it?"

"Do you think I can do it?" she asked doubtfully.

"Honey, I know you can. You've got that chin, remember, and all the Durant spunk, plus whatever your dad bequeathed. You'll do fine."

"Do I tell her tonight or do you think it might upset her?" The adrenalin flooding her system at the news of Hesty's need for her almost balanced her reaction to her own accident and she was trembling on the edge of her seat as she peered anxiously at Thad.

"Tell her, by all means. It'll be the best medicine you could give her, you wait and see."

And with that, he drove on, leaving Lyle to her thoughts. By the time she had directed Thad where to take her luggage and spoken gravely to Ethel and Pam, she had more or less decided on the tack she would take with Hesty.

In the emergency, Ethel had given up her small first floor suite of rooms to the invalid and Lyle tiptoed apprehensively back to the slightly drafty, but surprisingly cheerful bedroom.

"You awake?" she peered diffidently at the slight mound on the enormous bed. "I'm back."

"Come in, come in, young'un. Step here in the light so I can see you." The rusty old voice had lost much of its vigor but none of its testiness and Lyle breathed easier as she moved to the side of the bed.

"Hi. You didn't behave very well while I was gone, did you?" she asked gently.

"If you'da had them two silly fools to put up with, you wouldn'a behaved none too good, yourself. Now, set here an' tell me what you been up to. Get yourself a feller while you was gone?"

"No, not a feller. I did get myself a great-aunt, though, if she'll have me."

In the ensuing silence, Lyle could hear the low murmur of voices coming from the front of the house and the officious ticking of the alarm clock from atop the photo laden bureau.

"You're Putnam's, ain't you?" Hesty asked in a strange tone. "I knowed it in my heart, but my head's some slower. Ethel tried to tell me not three days ago and I was too headset to hear."

"You mean Ethel guessed?" Lyle was amazed, wondering what else went on beneath the housekeeper's grizzled head of curls. Of course, she knew the Durant family tree like she knew her own.

"Said to me, she did, Durants always comes home to roost, red ones and black ones alike. Thought she meant Medwin, and him a dirty brown—they're like that, these days, but time was they was either red or black. You're one, I'm t'other, child." There was a sudden flush of color against the withered cheeks and Lyle was alarmed to see a shimmer of tears.

"Are you all right, Hesty? Aunt Hesty?" Self-consciously, Lyle took the old hand in her own and leaned close to study her aunt's expression.

"Oh, don't take on so. I'll do for another spell, now we can put the last chapter to the story." She smiled up at Lyle. "That's done me more good than a little, girl. Go 'long now and send Ethel to me. We'll talk tomorrow."

Thad was waiting, looking both tired and anxious. He led her into the living room as Ethel hurried away and Pam headed for the kitchen to make coffee.

"Here, sit down, you look ready to drop," he urged, leading her over to the sofa and seating himself beside her. "How did she take it?"

Lyle was silent, thoughtful for a moment. "You know, she wasn't really surprised. She mentioned something about Ethel's giving her a hint. It was strange."

Thad picked up one of her hands, playing idly with her fingers. "When you're that close to the other side, Lyle, I don't think there are too many surprises. Knowledge has a way of seeping through."

"She didn't say much," Lyle said doubtfully.

"She couldn't, not tonight. It's been a hard day and Hesty knows she has to save her strength, but there's tomorrow. She'll keep you pretty well tied down for the next few days asking all sorts of questions about your mother and granddad. Feel up to it?"

"Not at the moment, but I will when the time comes. I can't tell her much about my grandfather. Julia called him George—not called him, but referred to him, you know. George Putnam—George P.—that's all we knew of his name, but Julia's mother had told her about him when she was a girl. The funny thing is, I don't know much more about Julia—my own mother, than I do about him. Of course, I could find out from the fan magazines," she laughed and there was a high, thin edge to her laughter that brought a frown to Thad's face.

He took both her hands in his and pulled her around to face him. "Look here, Lyle, you're going to have to pull yourself together. Right now!" She stared at him, her eyes almost black with overstretched emotions. "Listen to me, it's been just hours since you were tossed about in a wreck and before that you were in another one, a far more tragic one that killed both your parents. Do you hear me, Lyle? Stop it!" He shook her as she struggled to turn away from him. "You've got to face it, Lyle. You've been running away from this thing and now, whether you're ready or not, it's caught up with you. For Hesty's sake, for your own sake, you've got to face it and go on from there."

Lyle started to talk. She talked about Reade and Julia, about their extraordinary talent, their celebrated good-looks and the overwhelming popularity that made friends of every acquaintance.

"She was so beautiful, Thad. Her hair was red, too, but a glowing sort of maroon. People thought it was dyed, but it wasn't."

Thad had his doubts about that but he was silent, letting her ramble on about her larger-than-life parents. After awhile he asked quietly, "And did they make you happy, Lyle? Did you share in their triumphs?"

"Oh, yes. No. Oh, I don't know, Thad!" She twisted away unhappily. "I made *them* so unhappy. Not unhappy, maybe, but—well, can you imagine how they felt when they had to introduce me to any of their friends? A great gawky carrottop who turned every color in the rainbow and couldn't manage to say hello without scuffing a hole in the carpet? In the first place, they looked far too young to have a daughter who looked grown up, even at fourteen, and there wasn't a single thing about me they could be proud of, Thad, not one! I was dirt plain and I couldn't carry a tune in a bucket!"

"Mere prettiness has nothing to do with beauty, Lyle, but all right, so you can't sing and you have freckles. Anything else to add to the list while we're purging? We'll forget your lamentable lack of fashion sense, because I've pretty well figured out the reason for that. You tried to disguise yourself, hide your youth, hoping nobody would ask questions about a young girl who was willing to hide herself away in the woods with two old women."

Lyle was silent, too emotionally spent to argue.

"Listen to me now. You're through feeling sorry for yourself. You're your own person now, Lyle, independent of your past. It doesn't matter what your parents wanted you to be, Lyle. If you can accept a dose of Eastern philosophy, consider that according to the laws of karma, you *chose* to be born in the circumstances you did because there was a debt to be paid, or something to be learned, perhaps." He was stroking her wrist with a long, square-tipped finger, sending currents flowing up her arm. "There's no knowing who owed whom, or who taught whom, if you had fit into your parents show business life, you'd be a different person, now wouldn't you? You probably wouldn't have ended up down here, for one thing." He grinned down at her and she felt her heart flip-flop in her breast at the warmth that flowed out from his golden hazel eyes.

"I—I don't think I'd have liked living in Beverly Hills."

"Somehow, I can't picture you there, either, honey.

So how do we know that things haven't worked out for you the way they were meant to? If there's a karmic debt to be worked out between you and Reade and Julia, there's no hurry. You'll meet in lifetime after lifetime, according to the beliefs of a large portion of the world's population, and eventually you'll reconcile your differences. The point is, you're separate entities. You have to work out your own destiny in the long run, just as they had to work out theirs, and you can't judge yourself by their standards. It's up to you to forgive *them* if they were too wrapped up in their own lives to have time for you. It was their loss, even if it wasn't your gain. If you can forgive and move on to the next step, you'll be on the way to becoming the person you were meant to be. Hold on to that bitterness and it will corrode you inside. Do you understand what I'm trying to tell you?"

Numbly, Lyle nodded. "I think so. At least, it feels right. Thad, I need more time. All this has been too much."

"I know, honey. I suspect you've had a pretty miserable time of it and now all this business today. It will come out all right, I promise you, and I'll be here if you need someone to hang onto, or to take a poke at, OK?"

"OK," she agreed shakily, hoarding the warmth of his hands against the time when she'd be alone with her thoughts.

"By the way, I brought in the other stuff from your car. You got your bag and the rest of it is in the hall, including all the evidence of your festive holiday."

"What evidence?" she asked, bewildered.

"The evidence that a lonely, miserable little girl had nothing better to do than wander up and down the

beach collecting literature from all the tourist shops,"
he said softly, almost breaking her up again.

"Oh, Thad, stop it!" she cried, laughing shakily.

"Stop what?"

"Stop being so kind to me! You told me to quit being
sorry for myself and if you're going to go on like that, I
don't think I can stand it!"

"Well, all right, Elsie Dinsmore, if you get all choked
up inside, remember all the times when you've wanted
to remove my head from my neck, hmm?" He pressed
a fist up under her chin and raised her face to his, then
with a look almost of resignation, he covered her lips
and drew her close against him. What started out as a
simple kiss of comfort suddenly took on a different
feeling as her lips parted for his probing exploration.
With a whispered oath, he put her abruptly away from
him and when she would have held him close to her
again, he stood up and waved her a brisk salute.

"You're going to make it now, aren't you?"

Lyle steeled herself against her own treacherous
weakness; he was only trying to comfort her, after all.
"Oh, I'm fine now, except that I feel like I've been
taken apart and put back together a few too many times
in the past few hours. Promise you won't be so nice to
me the next time we meet. It's not—not natural!" she
said with a brittle smile.

If Hesty accepted the news of a newly discovered
niece with equanimity, Ethel's acceptance was even
more perfunctory. She nodded her gray head several
times and said sourly that now she supposed Lyle would
be complaining about the leaks in her room, now that
she was kin instead of just hired.

Pam, the last to be told, had simply stared at her for

several minutes, then declared, "Well, I don't guess you're any better or worse than the rest of the crop. That makes four of us now, unless you've got a few more surprises for when things get dull around here."

"No, there's only me," Lyle replied soberly. She went on to tell Pam the bare essentials of her parentage, knowing it would be easier on this night of confession than later.

Pam had continued to stare at her, but with a different expression. Lyle was not at all sure the names, Camden and Durant, in that context, would have any meaning for her, for Pam did not strike her as either a concert goer or a television fan, but evidently, she was mistaken.

"Good heavens," she said softly, almost reverently. "I can hardly wait till mother hears about this! She's looked down her nose at the Durants as long as I can remember. *Her* people were literary, doncha know, Grandad Snavely went broke trying to peddle bad poetry in a fancy book he insisted on putting out every three years. Used up all the money his newspaper made and everything his own wife had, but he insisted on educating the masses up to his standard. Lord! Wait till I tell her about this, she'll probably want to put out a book on what it means to be related to Camden and Durant. She'll be claiming them both within six weeks, if I know her."

"It won't be the first time it's been considered," Lyle told her, laughing at Pams' irreverent views of her family. It was some time later when she realized that there was no bitterness involved at all in the idea of cashing in on Reade and Julia's fame—she must have truly exorcized all the sycophants up to and including Stan.

As Pam had hands like sledgehammers, according to Hesty, and Ethel was a sniveling old fool, the nursing, as Thad had predicted, fell largely to Lyle. Her deft, quiet manner seemed to soothe the old woman who grew testier every day as her health improved. Invalidism did not suit her at all and she complained bitterly at what she called mollycoddling.

"Rub some of that eau de cologne on my back, Lyle," she ordered, pronouncing it you-de-cologne. "Danged if I won't have holes in my back by the time that doctor lets me get up, the young upstart!"

The young upstart, who must have been almost fifty, came twice a day at first, then once, and as time went by, took to dropping in whenever he was in the neighborhood. Hesty was still not allowed company other than family, but as Thad so designated himself, he was a frequent visitor. His manner with the irascible old woman was both gentle and teasing and at first, Lyle always managed to be nearby when he came to visit.

It was almost three weeks after Hesty's attack when Lyle realized Thad was avoiding her. His manner was perfectly natural as long as they were not alone together, but should he come upon Lyle by herself, he always made some excuse to hurry off. Try as she would, she could think of no way in which she might have angered him.

It was perplexing. Not only that, it was distinctly uncomfortable. Did he think, for goodness sake, that she might have misinterpreted his kindness when he brought her back home after Christmas? He had kissed her a few times and had gone out of his way to help her on more than one occasion but surely he didn't think she would be so foolish as to . . .

Well, she could be just as cool as he could! In fact, she could be conveniently absent whenever he dropped by. It took a little managing and once, after successfully avoiding him for almost a week, she scurried out the back door just as he elbowed his way into the kitchen with his arms full.

"Hey, wait up, will you? Take this bird. Berthalee baked it for Hes and the damned thing has leaked all over me."

There was a damp spot on his shirtfront and Lyle tried to suppress a smile at his dismay. "It won't hurt you, you know. Chicken broth is supposed to be good for what ails you."

"Internally, not applied with a poultice. Hand me a towel, will you? Where are you running off to in such a rush? You're never around anymore."

"Oh, I'm here, just busy." He seemed out of sorts and it gave her a small sense of satisfaction. Sauce for the goose!

"Remember when you said if ever I needed you, you'd be willing to help me?"

Suspiciously, she looked up from the table where she was securing the foil around the hen. The memory of her words spoken Christmas day came back to her. "I remember. Why?"

Instead of answering right away, Thad stood there and watched as her deft hands tucked the wrap under the chicken. She was wearing her oldest dress, as she had spent most of the morning transferring the remainder of Hesty's things from her old room, and her hair was tousled from reaching to the backside of the closet. In fact, she looked a complete wreck, as far as grooming was concerned, which suited her just fine. At least he wouldn't think she had designs on him. She blew upward as a curl fell across her face.

"Well, I need you," he replied, reaching out to tuck the hair behind her ear. His hand lingered and she looked up at him, acutely conscious of his touch. Oddly enough, he seemed to have lost his train of thought, for he simply stood there, looking almost bemused.

"What do you need me for?" she asked impatiently. No, it wasn't impatience in her voice, but just as well to let him think that breathless note was because she was rushed and in a hurry to hear him out.

"Oh—what? This stuff is alive, isn't it? I told you that that first night when you were sneaking about in the yard."

"I was *not* sneaking about! Please leave my hair alone and get on with it. I don't have all day, you know."

"As to that, you'll have more time from now on. Doc Titus finally got hold of a nurse. Mauncey Midgette can come from eight until two starting day after tomorrow."

"But we don't need a nurse," Lyle cried, dismayed.

"Of course you do. You're run ragged, Lyle, trying to look after Hesty and do most of the housework, too."

"Ethel and Pam do that," she asserted.

"Ethel and Pam are supposed to do it but it's obvious that Ethel spends more time nursing her ailments and Pam's chasing after Zeb and Johnny morning, noon and night. You can't do everything yourself, Lyle, even granting your willingness. You were just beginning to fill out a little and now you look like a walking scarecrow, shadows under your eyes, bones sticking out, keep on this way and Titus'll have two of you on his hands."

"Thank you for your kind words, Mr. Creed," she said sarcastically. "You're a great ego builder! For your information, I've never been chubby, and as for any imagined shadows, well—oh, leave me alone! I've got to get this hen in the refrigerator and then I have to—"

He interrupted, "Yes, and then you have to sit down and have a cup of coffee with me while I tell you how you're going to get me out of a tight spot. You promised, remember?"

"I don't think it's particularly becoming of you to insist like that," she replied feelingly.

"If you go on being so damned stubborn, I'm forced to insist. I'm not particularly known for my niceness whenever I want something." He moved with a lean, easy grace to take down two mugs and Lyle slammed the refrigerator door and crossed to the stove.

"You'll have to make do with instant," she said aggressively.

"Fine with me," he countered easily.

"All right, what do you need from me?" she demanded.

"My, aren't we gracious?" he teased, and went on to explain his dilemma. He had invited several people for dinner Friday night and now his housekeeper was called away on a family emergency. He needed someone to fill the gap.

"But I'm not sure I can do it," she faltered.

"Nothing to it. Berthalee's freezer has everything you'll need. Just put it together on time—you know the sort of thing that's needed. There'll only be six of us."

She looked at him doubtfully, seeing the golden

lights glinting in his hazel eyes. Darn the man! Why couldn't she have continued to avoid him?

"Oh, come on, Lyle, it's no big deal. Just a matter of thawing and cooking, putting a few festive touches on the old place, and of course, serving—" He cocked a wicked brow at her and Lyle's spirits plunged as she realized the role in which he had cast her. "—as hostess." He grinned wickedly, and she could have hit him! He knew exactly what had gone through her mind in those few seconds, as if he were twisting the dials and manipulating her emotions for his own amusement.

"I'm not at all certain I want to be your hostess. I'm sure you have someone else who could do a better job."

"But I've asked you. You're handy, you can run back and forth between here and there to see to all those little last-minute things women always fuss over and furthermore, Miss Camden, you owe me a favor, if I may be so crass as to bring it up."

"Oh, all right. Friday, you say." She considered possible excuses she might make, knowing full well nothing would keep her from the chance to play hostess to his host. Still, pride insisted on its due and she informed him that *if* the nurse worked out and *if* Hesty had no objections and *if* nothing happened between now and then, she'd be glad to do what she could.

"And *if*, my prickly little cactus, you decide to back out on our bargain, you'll be red in more places than you imagined possible." He grinned as the color flooded her face.

The advent of Mauncey Midgette into the household had a calming effect on everyone. Mauncey was a large woman in her forties and she managed to treat Hesty with a fine mixture of authority and respect in a way that had the invalid agreeing easily to a regimen Lyle had despaired of ever imposing.

"She done me legs a sight o' good," Ethel pronounced with satisfaction the first afternoon, displaying a pair of dense elastic stockings. "Long as she stays outten my kitchen, we'll get along." Which after only one day, was high praise indeed from Ethel Tarr.

Lyle had taken advantage of the fact that Thad was visiting Hesty to run over to his house and survey the situation. After a quick glance in the bulging freezer, she was able to come up with an easy, delicious menu, and then she walked into the living room with an eye to deciding on the floral arrangements.

Lost in admiration of the excellent proportions and the exquisite furnishings, it was some time before she got down to her appointed task. The ceilings were high, stark white and laced with heavy beams that matched the satiny nut-brown paneling. Instead of the more expected early American furnishings, Thad had chosen several fine oriental rugs, a pair of sofas done in a brick red, black and gold chintz, their down-filled cushions fairly shouting comfort, and a fascinating assortment of antique and handcrafted things. Flowers would have been acceptable, but an idea began to take shape in her mind and she went back to the pantry to look over the containers, thinking in terms of the abundant variety of greenery instead of flowers.

Thad was just leaving when Lyle got back to the Knob and, responding to his lifted eyebrow, she gave him a thumbs up sign, hurrying on inside before he could waylay her.

On the morning of the party, Pam looked into her

bedroom as she was putting the finishing touches on her hair before going down for breakfast.

"Got a minute? Could I ask you something?"

"Of course. What is it?"

"It's about tonight—this party thing. You see, Thad's invited me to go with Zeb and—"

"Zeb?" Lyle asked, surprised. "I would have thought Johnny."

"Mmmm. Well, you see, Johnny's sort of in the doghouse at the moment. Remember that night I didn't get in until so late? Johnny and I had been trying out one of the overhauled engines on the *Gale* and I mentioned something about the new harbor works at Wanchese and—well, we just sort of—went." She shrugged.

"To Wanchese?"

"Yep. Johnny radioed Zeb to tell him we were going and as soon as he had contacted him and told him not to expect us back till later, he cut the radio off—sort of mid-splutter, you might say. Zeb was furious!"

"But I still don't see what Thad has in mind asking you and Zeb. Unless he's looking for fireworks."

"Oh, Zeb and Thad are old buddies. Zeb's a few years younger, but they've always gotten along better than Thad and Johnny. They're a lot alike, you know, both grim and hard when anything doesn't suit them. Johnny's a doll, a real load of fun, but then, he's always had Zeb right on his heels if he didn't shape up."

"Well, so you're going with Zeb. What did you need to ask me?"

"The thing is, I'm not all that up on what one wears out in polite society. I mean, if it's more formal than jeans and best t-shirts, I'm lost."

Lyle felt a laugh bubble up. The idea of being asked to advise someone on fashion was faintly ludicrous, considering the way she had dressed ever since she had been there. Not that she dressed that much smarter before, having always had the feeling she should dress to be invisible as much as possible, but at least she had been exposed to what Pam called polite society.

"Are you sure you want me to advise you?"

"Who else? Ethel, maybe? Even if you do look sort of frumpy, yourself, at least you have an idea of what's proper at a thing like this. I mean, your parents—"

"Oh, yes, my parents," Lyle replied, her amusement fading as she realized Pam was honestly at a loss. So the careless khaki shorts, the hiking boots and the slightly dated hippy look were not deliberate. Lyle had thought she honestly didn't care enough to invest in a few smart dresses and a pair or two of nylons.

"Well, first we'd better see what we have to work with," she ventured, going to Pam's closet.

The half an hour that followed grew more and more hilarious as the two girls compared their meager wardrobes, each laughing as much at herself as at the other.

"Bad case of the blind leading the halt, if you ask me," Pam declared after trying on Lyle's best gray flannel. The color did absolutely nothing for her faded tan and medium brown hair.

"Pam, if you'd let me take up the waist of the lavender and then try it without the sweater underneath, it would look loads better. It's really quite a nice dress, only—"

"Only I seem to make everything I put on look like it's been through the mill. You can't do much when you travel with a pack instead of a suitcase, but do you really think it might look better?" She held the dress up to her, nipping the waist in doubtfully. "It's kind of low in the neck, isn't it?"

"A little cleavage never hurt anybody," Lyle decreed cheerfully.

"I don't think I have enough to cleave."

"Stop trying to be modest," Lyle teased. "We're built almost exactly alike, so whatever you say goes double."

"You've got a figure, at least. Sometimes I think Zeb and Johnny look on me as another boy. That's why I wear the long dresses, I guess—lest they forget." Her grin brought a flash of piquancy to her features and Lyle was emboldened to suggest something more.

"Why don't you let me trim up your hair? It's really a lovely shade. All it needs is shaping up a bit to bring out the lines of your neck and your cheekbones and eyes."

"Look who's talking! I suppose you're going to screw yours up in a hard knot again," Pam said disdainfully.

"I might surprise you. I bought a dress Christmas— something sort of different, and maybe I'll do my hair another way."

They went to Lyle's room then and she dug out the dress box from the back of her closet where it had resided since she came home from that ill-fated trip. Fortunately, the silk jersey material wasn't crushed and its folds flowed beautifully as she held it up for Pam's approval.

"Oh, Lyle, that's gorgeous! Almost the color of pistachio ice cream!"

Lyle giggled. "More like pea soup. Do you suppose everyone will think I'm losing my marbles if I come slinking out in this?"

"After wearing those drab horrors ever since you got

here, you probably couldn't slink if you tried! Maybe you'd better practice."

Lyle located a needle and thread and set to work refitting Pam's dress, reveling in the warm friendship she had missed so much since leaving Carol.

"This will do wonders for you, properly nipped in to show off your waist and without that sweater," she assured the younger girl.

"Yeah, it'll freeze my gizzard off, for starters. Old Zeb might sit up and take notice, though. And so will Thad when he gets a look at you in that silky thing."

"Don't be silly! As long as the house looks all right and the food is good, Thad won't notice what I'm wearing," Lyle protested, all the time wondering if he *would* notice. She resolved to spend as long as it took to get her hair in some semblance of order for tonight, and not by the simple expedient of twisting it into a tight knot on top of her head, for a change!

"Yeah, I hear you talking," Pam derided. "I suppose you won't notice him, either, in those slim tailored pants and a shirt that practically rips across his shoulders."

"How do you know what he'll be wearing?" Lyle asked, nipping off a thread with her teeth.

Pam stretched her arms up over her head and slanted a mischievous look through the window to the half hidden house further down the road. "Oh, just psychic, I guess. Seriously, Lyle, did you ever see him when he didn't look good enough to eat with a spoon? I mean, there's just something about him—sex appeal, I guess. Too bad he looks on me as a kid sister."

Chapter Six

It was not unlike playing with a dollhouse she had as a child, but there was an added element that Lyle tried to ignore. She had been unable to resist caressing the already gleaming furniture with a soft cloth, had put the shrimp cocktails in to chill, readied the oyster casserole for the oven and done all the other last-minute jobs.

Before she returned to the Knob to bathe and dress, she began one last bowl of greenery. There were already several handsome arrangements scattered around the house, but it had occurred to her only minutes ago that a bowl of holly, pine and wax myrtle would look lovely against the old brass platter on the entrance table.

Ouch! She sucked her pricked finger as she wrestled with the stem of holly and wished for a heavier frog. The only one she had found was almost too small for the thick stems and she was having to balance them precariously. There—now the pine was slipping again—it was topheavy, but such a luxurious spray.

Biting her lip, she leaned over and peered down through the greenery for a hole to poke the stubborn branch into and almost knocked the whole arrangement off the cabinet when someone spoke behind her. She jerked around, aware at the same time of the toppling holly branch, and grabbed for it. Too late, she felt it tangle in her hair. "Why don't you watch what you're doing?" she cried out in vexation.

"I'd rather watch what you're doing," Thad replied, obviously amused at her plight.

"Well now you've really fixed it! There, the whole thing has fallen apart, I hope you're satisfied!"

He threw back his head and laughed. "You look like some ancient, enraged diety, complete with laurel wreath and scepter."

Some of her anger faded as she visualized what she must look like with the holly tangled in her topknot, a stem of pine in her hand and masses of greenery scattered on the cabinet before her. The word, altar, for cabinet, came to her mind and the last vestige of irritation slipped away as she joined him in laughter.

"Oh, darn you! Everything was all ready, too, except for this last arrangement."

"It looks beautiful, Lyle. I don't think the place has ever breathed so freely before—looks as if someone lives here."

"Well," she replied in surprise, "someone does. Look, will you please get this mess out of my hair? I've got it all to clean up now."

"Hmm, I'm not so sure," he murmured, gently untangling the prickly leaves from her untidy hair. Then, seeing her puzzled expression he added, somewhat abstrusely, "Live here, that is. Hold still, there, that's got it."

Still, he didn't release his hold on her head. After dropping the released branch to the floor, he clasped her face and tilted it toward him, a smile lighting his eyes before it ever touched his mouth.

"It's like glowing coals, isn't it?" he asked softly, his breath playing warmly over her still face. "I can't help but wonder if there's anything to the promise or if you're really the little pilgrim you make out to be." His eyes dropped, to roam the length of her body, making her acutely conscious of her rumpled denim dress.

"Promise?" she breathed, her voice barely audible to her own ears over the racing pulse.

"The promise of your navy blue eyes. Somewhere I remember reading that people with dark blue eyes were the most passionate of all. And there's your hair, so warm and vital, and your mouth that trembles so temptingly. Ah, Lyle Camden, just what are you up to, hmmm? Are you trying to drive me quietly crazy?"

His hands dropped to her shoulders, then continued on down to her hips to pull her against him as he leaned his forehead against her hair. "Just when I have you all figured out, first as a dried-up spinster, then as a scared adolescent, you shift to something else. I keep seeing this redheaded angel peeping out at me, sticking her tongue out and defying me to chase her." He shook her slightly and she could see the powerful drumming of a pulse at the base of his throat.

"Did I mention that I'm about to kiss you within an inch of your life? Is that why you look so panicky, love? Is it me or is it men in general?"

When she didn't answer, couldn't answer, he leaned closer and covered her trembling lips with his own. She could feel the beat of their combined hearts shaking the earth as he drew her further and further into the kingdom of the senses. All thought of Stan and his perfidy was erased as she clung helplessly to the warm flesh of Thad's shoulders, allowing her hands to caress where they would.

He lifted his lips just far enough to capture her dazed eyes with his own and she watched the subtle, gleaming change that came over them as he deliberately covered her breast with a hard, exploring hand.

She stiffened, frightened by the flood of feeling that raced through her unprepared body, and he gentled her, as one might gentle a wild, untamed colt. "Easy, darling, I'm not going to hurt you," he whispered, studying her wide, bewildered eyes as his fingers traced the contours of her hardened nipple. "It's a natural thing you're feeling, Lyle, a womanly awakening that's come just a bit later for you than for most, but trust me—I promise I won't take you too far—too fast."

He whispered her name against her lips as if it were an endearment and she melted again, clinging to his hard, warm strength.

"Thad, darling, are you home?"

The moment shattered into a million brittle fragments as the clear, well modulated voice caroled through the house.

Lyle froze, scarcely aware that Thad's grip had tightened momentarily before he released her to stride away. She felt as if an Arctic wind had sprung up from nowhere.

Standing where he had left her, Lyle heard the greetings from the other room, Cora's mention of luggage, Thad's deep rejoinder and then she realized she was eavesdropping.

Escape through the back door? Even as she considered the move it was too late. Thad was ushering Cora

Lambert through the doorway, his enigmatic expression giving away nothing of his thoughts as he inclined his head to catch something the woman was saying.

Lyle's attention was on Cora when the older woman caught sight of her and she didn't miss the flicker of surprise as carefully groomed eyebrows climbed the alabaster brow.

"You remember Cora Lambert, don't you, honey? Cora, this is my fiancée, Lyle Camden. You met briefly in Manteo but you might not have seen her too clearly at the time."

There wasn't the slightest hesitation in Thad's voice as he made the introduction and for a moment, Lyle didn't take in the meaning of his words. By the time a protest had formed itself on her lips, she was aware of the silent plea on Thad's face. Before either of them could speak, however, Cora exclaimed, "Your fiancée! Darling, if you'd told me you'd stolen Hesty's domestic, I might have believed you, but I've known you a little too long, not to mention too well, to be taken in by your offbeat sense of humor." Her laughter was a beautifully produced piece of music that never once involved her eyes. Those dwelt coldly on Lyle, even as her beautifully manicured hand ran up Thad's shoulder to tug gently at his ear.

Darn her, Lyle thought. *I might have let him flounder around in deep water except that I won't give her the satisfaction.* She smiled up at Thad and said calmly, "I'd better get this mess cleared away, if you all will excuse me."

"Thanks, darling. Cora's come to visit for a few days and as Berthalee's not here, you're going to have to pinch-hit. You'll still be able to spend your days at the Knob, though, if you need to."

Where she got the breath to reply, Lyle couldn't have said, for events were piling up with a frightening rapidity, but in for a penny, in for a pound. "Of course, Thad. I'd have to be over here early in the morning, anyway, to clean up after tonight," she forced a small laugh, gesturing to the mess before her, "and speaking of cleaning up . . ."

"Great. I'll bring in Cora's bag and later on, I'll get your things from the Knob. You can have—well, you know which room is yours, don't you?" There was a decidedly wicked gleam in his eyes and Lyle wondered, feeling the color flood her face, just what she was letting herself in for.

She might still have backed out had not Cora spoken of the last time they had met.

"Well, if she really is your fiancée, as you claim, Thad, you'd better shorten the reins. The last time I saw her she was doing a spot of celebrating with a very special friend, but I don't suppose she told you about that, did she?" Honey dripped from every word and Lyle felt almost sickened by the insinuations. Whatever game Thad had been playing, she thought hopelessly, was all over now.

She had not bargained for Thad's handling of the situation. "I don't think we'll rehash old business if you don't mind, Cora. You know my feelings on that score, I'm sure."

No one could ignore the warning in Thad's cool words. Even Cora, for all her real or implied intimacy with Thad, was effectively silenced, more by something in his manner than by his actual words.

It was a strange dinner party. Johnny Burrus had been asked to round out the numbers, for to Lyle's surprise, Cora had not been an invited guest. There had been little time to talk to Thad privately, but while Cora relaxed in a hot soak, he ran her back to the Knob for her clothes.

"Look," he said in a slightly harried tone, "there isn't time to go into the whys and wherefores—I'm not sure you'd understand them anyway. In fact, I'm not at all certain I do, myself." His crooked smile bore a resemblance to the first sardonic grimace Lyle had seen the night she arrived at Frisco, and with a small shock, she wondered how she had ever thought him unattractive. The strength of his irregular features, the warmth that gleamed from his eyes far outweighed mere handsomeness.

"Someone will have to let Pam in on the plan. Zeb and Johnny, too, I suppose," Lyle said tentatively.

"Leave it to me. I'll tell everybody as much as they need to know while you scamper upstairs and grab your glad rags."

She smiled up at him impudently. "Prepare yourself. I have a new dress and it's not gray."

"Good grief, it's a good thing you warned me, although if I could propose to you after seeing you in nothing but those Orphan Annie outfits you run around in, anything will be an improvement!"

A little provoked, she replied tartly, "Well, it seemed a good idea at the time—to look older and more settled, that is. Anyway, if I embarrass you, you can always unpropose. I'm not at all sure why you did it in the first place."

"Oh, no, it's too late to wiggle out of it now. You backed me up like a veteran and I—well, as a matter of fact, I'm not sure just why I did pull a stunt like that. Let's say I wasn't quite ready to have Cora waltz back into my life as if she had never been gone." Thad's chin took on a more aggressive attitude and Lyle was suddenly aware of a welter of conflicting emotions, among them disappointment and an unreasonable jealousy of Cora Lambert who could bring on such strong feelings in a man she had dropped several years ago.

In a small voice, she asked him, "Couldn't you just tell her how you feel?"

"It's not that simple, I'm afraid. There's Cora's family, for one thing. This is a small village on a small island and the people who live here have been closely tied in one way or another for generations. Cora tends to be explosive and I don't want to upset matters with her parents, who are good friends of mine, or her sister, whose husband is a business associate."

"And you think it won't upset her to find you engaged to me?" Lyle asked incredulously. "I don't think she really believed you, anyway."

Thad leveled an enigmatic look at her, "And what about you, Lyle? Did you believe me?"

All the instincts of a lifetime rushed to Lyle's defense. It was suddenly painfully clear to her that she wanted more than anything in her life to be able to take Thad's proposal seriously. It was equally clear that it would be a fatal mistake. No man, given the choice between the exquisite Cora Lambert and plain Lyle Camden would hesitate, and no matter what Thad thought now, he would go back to Cora in the end.

"I believe you need to make Cora suffer just a part of what you must have suffered when she left you," she confided, reaching out to touch his arm with gentle fingers.

"I see you've been listening to the women's gossip," he said dryly. "Lyle—sometimes it takes a shock, an unexpected turn of events to make you stop and take stock of where you are, what you want out of life. You, of all people, should know that. Well, maybe I've been taking stock lately," he finished obliquely.

"And you think it's better to play a waiting game," she prompted.

Again she caught a look from those golden hazel eyes that she found impossible to interpret. His hand covered her own, which was still resting on his arm, and he said quietly, "A waiting game. Yes, under the circumstances, that would be wise, I believe."

She thought later that he had been surprised when she came downstairs in the soft green jersey dress. The styling was deceptively simple, the bodice draping in a manner that made the most of her femininity and the skirt swirling gracefully around her slender legs. Even Cora, she was secretly delighted to note, gave her a pretty thorough scrutiny before relegating her to the ranks of the unimportant.

By the time they were seated about the fire enjoying after-dinner coffee, Lyle knew it was not going to work. In the first place, Cora had not missed an opportunity to remind the other guests of her previous relationship with Thad, a task that had been devilishly simple due to the fact that Lyle was busy seeing to the serving and catering to the company while Cora was free to indulge in reminiscences. Before Lyle knew quite how it came about, Jerry and Phoebe Austin and Carlin and Anna Williams were prefacing most of their statements with, 'you and Thad, Cora,' or, 'remember when Thad and Cora . . .' or even, 'now that you're back, Cora. . . .'

Against that, Lyle didn't stand a chance. Thad had done his best, at first, standing beside her with an arm across her shoulders as they greeted the other two couples. He had introduced Lyle as his fiancée, ignoring the startled looks, but it had been Cora who had smoothly slipped in with suggestions that Lyle hang their coats in *her* room, since the other closets were crowded, and by the way, would she please stop by the kitchen and bring back a few more ashtrays.

There are certain feminine tricks that are completely outside the realm of masculine experience and Cora was a past mistress of the art. Even the patronizing way she referred to Lyle as Thad's little girl friend, and complimented her, saying that she had done just a wonderful job, hadn't she? brought a feeling of frustrated rage to Lyle, but she was too unsure of her ground to dare challenge the older woman.

The men were engrossed in discussions of boats and nets, the past shrimp season and the upcoming spring run of drum and as Pam was curled up beside Zeb engaging all his interest for the moment, Lyle was left to the tender mercies of the other women, who were old friends of Cora's.

Defiantly, Lyle suppressed her hurt, but when she saw an opportunity, she excused herself and crossed to where Johnny was serving himself another drink.

"Pam mentioned that you were interested in traditional Irish music," she said brightly. "Do you prefer the Boys of the Lough or the Bothy Band?"

They went on to discuss various recording groups and as Lyle caught Thad's lowering gaze on her, she resolutely turned her back. When Johnny noticed her all but empty glass, he asked her what she was drinking and crossed the room to get her a refill of ginger ale.

She took the opportunity to sneak a glance at Thad, only to meet his thunderous look. Carlin Williams had a hand on his shoulder and was obviously nearing the point of a long, involved story, but from the looks of it, Thad was not enjoying it very much. The metallic sheen in his eyes was leveled at Lyle and she felt their anger from all the way across the room.

Well, as far as she was concerned, she had done nothing to warrant his wrath. She had done *her* bit to maintain his pitiful little farce of an engagement and if he expected her to hang onto his arm and seduce him with her eyes, as Cora had done every chance she got, he had another think coming! She had been made a target for Cora's malicious comments enough as it was, without exposing herself to even more!

With a smile that was a good deal more welcoming than she intended, Lyle greeted Johnny as he held out her glass. She had made coffee earlier and Thad had brought in the heavy tray for her, placing it on the coffee table. It might have been accidental, it might have been planned, but Cora just happened to be sitting in a position to pour and without creating an unnecessary scene, Lyle had no choice but to let her. She herself, had refused a cup, saying she preferred something cold.

"What's your drink?" she asked Johnny now, as he sat beside her on the leather-covered window seat.

"Same as yours but with a dash of bourbon. Why, yours taste flat?"

Lyle laughed brightly. "As a matter of fact, it does. How about pumping it up for me?"

After that, the conversation grew gayer and gayer, with Pam and Zeb joining them after a prolonged trip to the kitchen.

Through it all, Lyle was aware of the stern looks of disapproval directed at her by Thad. These looks had the effect of making her wittier than she had been in her life and by the time the last good-bye was said, she was quite elated at her own social success.

"Cora, we'll excuse you while Lyle and I clear away the worst of the leavings," Thad said succinctly as soon as he closed the door.

"Oh, but I'm not a bit sleepy," Cora replied, stretching in a way that made the most of her tiny, but voluptuous figure.

"It's late and you'll feel better tomorrow if you get a good night's sleep. Lyle will serve breakfast whenever you want it."

Before Lyle could explode, Cora, her opaque eyes flickering back and forth between them, declared she'd like coffee about ten and then, "After that, we'll see. Really, though, darling, your little girl friend can clear away while I keep you company."

"Good-night Cora. We'll see you tomorrow," Thad said repressively.

Even Cora, in the face of such adamant discouragement, stepped down.

Lyle was on the point of excusing herself, knowing if she stayed a minute longer, she'd say something that would be better left unsaid, when Thad's hand tightened on her arm until she almost cried out. He propelled her into the kitchen and slammed the door behind them before spinning her around to face him.

"What do—?"

"Exactly what were you up to tonight?" Their lowered voices clashed, equally furious, and Thad's won.

"What was I up to? What do you think I was up to? I was cooking and serving and fetching ashtrays for your girl friend, that's what I was up to!"

"Keep your voice down! You know good and well what I'm talking about! You and Johnny, sitting there giggling at each other like a couple of fifteen year olds, so wrapped up in each other you ignored the other guests! I'm not in the habit of being made a fool of, Lyle Camden, and—"

"*You're* not! Well, for your information, I'm not in the habit of being an unpaid drudge! If you think calling me your fiancée for the evening will keep you from having to hire a replacement for your housekeeper, you're pretty dumb! A favor, you said, well, if that's—"

"When I pay for your services, I'll damned well see that I get them," he told her deliberately.

The cheerful turquoise countertops cluttered with the prosaic leavings from the party could have been a thousand miles away as they stood there, glaring at each other. Lyle was far too wrapped up in her own hurt disappointment to be aware of the baffled anger in Thad's face.

"Go to bed," he said tiredly. "This can wait until tomorrow. Just don't think for one minute I'm through with you, Lyle Camden. You haven't heard the last of this business."

Anger rushed back to overwhelm her momentary bewilderment and she stormed at him, "Just a darned minute, Thad Creed, what do you mean, you're not through with me? *I'm* through with *you*, do you hear me? You can take your old—your eight hour old engagement and—and, well, you know what you can do with it! I'm tired of jumping when you say jump and being yelled at if I don't jump high enough! I'm tired of Cora and her friends with their 'you and Cora, Thad,' and their 'remember when Thad and Cora did this,' and 'remember when Thad and Cora did that!' Well, as far as I'm concerned, Thad and Cora can hold hands and jump in the lake, because I hate you both!"

Her vision was blighted by a sudden shimmer of tears and she could not see the subtle change of expression that came over Thad's face. When he spoke, it was in a calm, almost silky voice instead of the rough growl he had flayed her with earlier.

"If I didn't know better, I'd say you were jealous."

"Jealous! Of you? You—you have to love someone to be jealous of them and I'd never in a million years—"

"Don't commit yourself so far into the future, Lyle," he interrupted smoothly. "Meanwhile, the engagement stands. I've told Hesty and everyone else about it and I'm not going to retract my statement the morning after I first announce it."

"Then I will! You must be crazy if you think I'm going to hang around and watch Cora tie you up in knots. If—if I had a ring, I'd throw it back in your face!" she choked.

"Keep your voice down, dammit!" he demanded harshly.

"I will *not* keep my voice down!"

"Then I'll just have to make you, won't I?"

Before she could help herself, he pulled her roughly into his arms and ground his mouth into hers. Vainly, she struggled, hating him, hating the brutality and pain he was inflicting on her. One of his arms was clamped across her shoulders, the hand twisted in her hair holding her helplessly open to the onslaught of his marauding mouth, and the other hand dropped to her hips to force her awareness of him as a man. Against all reason, she found herself responding to him, clinging to the hard warmth of his body as her arms crept under his jacket to pull him closer to her. She was not even aware of when he broke past the barrier of her angry determination, but when her lips parted to his probe, the tiny fluttery feeling in the pit of her stomach grew into a wild expectancy and she kissed him back with an unschooled ardor.

His kiss softened, became a pleading instead of a demand, seduction instead of force and she felt the strength in her lower limbs begin to dissolve.

"Don't let me interrupt anything," Cora said with a brittleness that ripped through Lyle's vulnerable body like a chain saw. "I just wanted something to drink. You must ask your girl friend not to use so much salt in the future, Thad—in case she happens to cook for you again."

How Lyle got to sleep that night she never knew. Her mind was a senseless whirl long after her head touched the pillow and perhaps it was only the unaccustomed delight of a comfortable bed, plus her undeniable weariness after weeks of doing double duty as both nurse and housekeeper that did the trick.

Whatever it was, she was thankful for the few hours of rest when she arrived at the Knob the next morning. She had seen neither Thad nor Cora and she was seething with frustration by the time she confronted Hesty.

"Set down, girl. You look like you swallowed a hard crab. Got no call to get so riled with a man like Thad a-courting you."

"Yes, well that's all you know," Lyle fumed. She was ready to pack in the whole affair after last night, and only her consideration for her great-aunt's condition prevented her from exploding. More calmly, she continued. "I expect it was a mistake to start with. Thad thought it might work, although I'm still not certain just what he had in mind. Anyway, I want out, and as soon as I see him, I'm going to let him know it."

"Child, if you think you're a-gonna tell Thad which way to jump, you're crazy. I've knowed him all his born days, thought to settle Pam with him for awhile, but she'd never do for him. No, that boy needs something else, and I'm glad to see he's done got over that other woman. Done me a sight of good, I can tell you, when he told me about the pair of you."

Dismayed, Lyle realized Thad had not told Hesty the true state of affairs. Had he deliberately misled her or had the old woman, in her desire to see the two families joined, misunderstood? And Pam—did she believe it was real, too? Oh, just wait until she saw him!

Before she could simmer down, Hesty was off on a rambling tale of some long ago happening that included names that Lyle had grown familiar with. She listened with half an ear at first, and then her own turbulent thoughts took over.

How could she get out of the mess she had landed herself in? After all her resolutions, how could she have been so foolish as to become a victim of her own feelings? If she had any sense at all, she'd put a thousand miles between her and the man who was becoming entirely too important to her, she warned herself, knowing full well it was too late for either time or distance to matter.

"Well, don't you have anything to say about it?" Hesty demanded irritably, calling Lyle's mind back to the present.

"I'm sorry, Hesty. I must have been dozing after a late night."

"Missing that good feather bed of mine, ain't you? I'll have to give the pair of you one for a wedding present."

"May I come in?" Thad asked, poking his head around the door. Lyle started up from her chair, then settled back down. Darned if she would let him chase her away until she was good and ready to go.

"Come in, come in, son. I was just a-tellin' Lyle that I'd give you one of my feather beds for a weddin' present."

Thad's laugh moved like flickering fingers down her spine. Lyle was furious to hear him accept Hesty's offer gravely, telling her how much they would both enjoy it. Her lips clamped together in a straight line and she glared at him, hating the mocking devils of light that glinted back at her from his eyes.

"Got a proposition for you, gal of mine," he announced cheerfully, just as if last night's confrontation had never occurred.

"I think, if you don't mind, I've had enough of your propositions," she bristled.

He laughed again. Really, the man seemed to be in an abominably cheerful mood this morning! "Feisty, isn't she, Hes? Reminds me of my favorite Durant woman. Pity you wouldn't have me, old doll, then I wouldn't have to make do with second best."

Hesty cackled, gnarled old hands clapping together as if it were the best joke she'd heard in ages.

"Don't you want to know what it is I'm proposing, Lyle?" he asked, the wicked expression on his face giving the lie to his bland words.

"Not particularly. I'm not really interested in anything you have to suggest, if you want to know the truth."

"Wed her and bed her, she'll be a better woman for it," Hesty chuckled, causing the hated flames to consume Lyle's face again.

Lyle sat stiffly in the bedside chair, with Thad seated casually on Hesty's bed. He dropped a hand on her twisting fists, soothing them with small strokes as he grinned down at her. "Nevermind, sweetheart, we shouldn't tease you this way. You're rather irresistible, you know, when you go all stiff and fiery that way."

Gasping at his audacity, even knowing it was for Hesty's benefit, Lyle pulled her hands away and stood up, an action, unfortunately, that brought her far too close to him. He took advantage of the closeness, as she might have known he would, and pulled her to his side as he spoke to Hesty.

"Zeb's bought Lance Gaskill's small inboard and while the weather holds, we're going to run over to Ocracoke and bring it back."

"Better look to see that hired boy of Lance's ain't pulled the screws outten her. He'd steal the chickens from his own henhouse."

"I don't think I—" Lyle began, but she was interrupted.

"We'll be leaving in a few minutes. I thought Lyle might need to borrow a pair of Pam's jeans."

Lyle went, of course. It had been inevitable, considering Thad's deliberate timing. He knew full well she couldn't refuse in front of Hesty without answering some awkward questions. Hesty had regained a great deal of strength; nevertheless, there was a transparency about her that worried Lyle, and she knew Thad was more concerned than he really admitted.

The air was unusually clear and cold as they gathered in front of the Knob, and Lyle was glad of the jeans, though she wished she looked as delectable in them as Cora did in the tight black pants and fur windbreaker. Thad opened the passenger door and looked at Lyle with an imperceptible nod, but before she could move, either to the front or the back, Cora had slipped deftly under Thad's arm with a murmured thanks and seated herself in the front seat.

Leaning back against the rich upholstery on the five mile drive, Lyle resolved to show Thad that she was not his to order about. He might bring pressure to bear on her when they were in Hesty's presence, but outside the Knob, Lyle was free to act as she saw fit, and at the moment, she saw fit to enjoy her outing, Thad or no Thad.

Chapter Seven

The Shearwater was throbbing impatiently to be off when Thad pulled up to the docks at Hatteras. Lyle was slightly disappointed to learn that the throbbing was caused by the pumping of the bilges, for it somehow lessened the romantic appeal of the sleek, white cruiser, but she quickly recovered at the sight of the activity.

A small, open boat loaded with nets was gliding in through the breakwater and several men were shoveling fish from still another boat as Lyle stepped out to inhale the pungent aroma of fish and fuel oil and salt water.

She shivered in the black turtleneck sweater and jeans, but after seeing how trim and almost attractive she looked in the outfit, she had refused to cover it with her tweed coat. It still chaffed her ego, that Cora had slipped into the front seat and that Thad, with a mocking glance at his supposed fiancée, had let her.

Johnny jumped up from the cockpit of the cruiser as she let herself out of the backseat and at the sight of her, he gave an appreciative whistle. That went a long way toward soothing Lyle's fragile self-confidence and she sniffed at Thad and Cora and hurried over to where he waited to assist her aboard.

"As much as I hate to cover up such attractive scenery, love, you'd better put on this oilskin before we take off."

Lyle took the yellow slicker with a cheeky grin and followed Johnny on a Cook's tour of the boat.

"After we get going, I'll take you forward and we can watch the bottom as we head toward the inlet," he promised.

"You mean you can see it? Is it shallow? Are there fish?"

"It's not exactly the Caribbean, you little dunce, but you might see a shell or two, maybe a hard crab." He grinned at her and pushed her gently down on one of the seats as Thad and Pam cast off. Cora was nowhere in sight and Lyle presumed she had gone inside the compact blue and white cabin.

The sound of the engines changed pitch and they slid away from the docks, heading out past the breakwater to the channel. Pam took her place beside Zeb at the wheel and Thad, Johnny and Lyle stood slightly behind them, watching the small flock of gulls that swooped after them in search of handouts.

"Stomach all right this morning?" Johnny asked over the sound of the engines. He turned to Thad and grinned. "I have a feeling I introduced your gal to hard liquor last night, old fellow. Didn't know she was a complete neophyte until she tossed back a swig and almost strangled. Took to it like a duck in water after that, though."

Lyle, catching the look on Thad's face, could have

killed him! She would just as soon not be reminded of
last night. It seemed she had made even more of a fool
of herself than she had thought.

"I didn't do anything too silly, did I?" she asked
Johnny, ignoring Thad as best she could.

"You were a perfect peach, honey. Hospitality
personified."

Delight suddenly bubbled up through her apprehen-
sions and Lyle thought, oh, Johnny, you're a devil! And
I'm in just the right mood to play along with you.

Cora appeared in the hatchway and seemed to be
beckoning to Thad, who was glaring off to the side.
Lyle followed his look and exclaimed, "Oh, are those
pelicans?"

"I'm sure Johnny would be delighted to give you the
rundown on all the birds and the—" Thad began
grimly.

"And the fish," Lyle finished for him, glancing up
provocatively before following Johnny up to the bow
where they stretched out on the deck to watch the
bottle-green water flow past the sharp white prow. For
some reason she felt more alive than she had in ages
and she was firmly determined to make the most of
today's excursion.

Ten minutes later, she sensed Thad's presence behind her. He seemed to be radiating a fierce sort of
vibration that affected every nerve in her body.

"Your face is going to be raw," he told her curtly. "I
think you've had enough of this wind."

"But there isn't any wind. It's perfectly calm," she
declared perversely.

"Then what's making your hair fly back like a small
craft warning? Come on, Lyle, you'd better come
below now."

"When I'm ready to come below, I will, thank you. I do know enough to come in out of the rain, you know."

Without a word, he turned and moved swiftly along the side of the cabin to drop down to the deck level. For several minutes after he left, Lyle remained silent. She was uncomfortably aware of her burning face now that he had mentioned it. The tissue-thin skin that went with her sort of hair did not take kindly to the elements, as she should know. It was pure stubbornness on her part that made her defy him.

"You know what you're doing, I suppose," Johnny remarked quietly.

"What do you mean? My face? So it will be a little bit chapped, so what? It certainly won't be the first time," she declared airily.

"That's not what I mean and you know it."

"Thad, I guess you mean."

"Thad you *know* I mean. He's livid."

"Well, it's nothing to him if my skin gets blown clear off my face!"

"Only that you're engaged to him and if you were engaged to me, my little hotshot, I'd turn you across my knee."

"Oh, Johnny!" she gurgled, "You can't convince me that you'd play the heavy. You'd never settle down to one girl long enough to wield that much authority."

"Pam been talking?" He grinned crookedly, an almost smug expression on his attractive young face.

"Ethel, as a matter of fact."

"That old biddy! For all she stays in the kitchen all day long, there's damned little that gets by her beady eyes."

Lyle rolled over on her back, staring up at the sky. It was cobalt with a veil of white chiffon drawn over it and the chiffon was gathered into tiny knots along the western edge. "If he wants to boss someone around, let him look after Cora's tender complexion. At her age, she needs all the help she can get."

"Meow."

"Sorry. That was dreadful of me. For some reason, she seems to bring out the worst in me. Because she's so beautiful, I suppose."

"She's that, all right, but considering what was between her and Thad before you came along—before Lambert came along, too, for that matter, you'd react that way if she looked like a halloween mask. Only natural, women being women."

"And you're the expert, of course."

"Research, m'dear, pure, unselfish, dedicated research. I'd take her off his hands for you if I were a few years older or she were a few months younger."

"Don't do it on my account, thanks. Anyway, she's not nice enough for you, regardless of ages. You deserve someone really super, in spite of your rakish pretensions." Lyle wrinkled her nose in a grin, then winced as the tender skin protested.

"Ah ha! Hurts, doesn't it? If you won't do it for your dearly beloved, you'll sure enough go below for me, sweet potato. Come on, now. Hop up, and don't tumble overboard, for Pete's sake. The tide this close to Hatteras Inlet is so swift it would hardly be worthwhile to pick you up. Burn too much fuel chasing you down."

"I'm all right, really."

"Sure you are, Rose Red, only you've got my only spare slicker on and it'll get rough in a minute. I'm not about to lose a perfectly good slicker just because you want to get back at your honey for playing in somebody else's yard."

"Nag, nag, nag!" She held out her hands to be pulled to her feet, conscious once she had steadied herself of Thad's dark, closed face behind the windscreen.

By the time they cruised into Silver Lake, the sheltered harbor cupped in the middle of Ocracoke Village, Lyle's face was on fire, but nothing would make her acknowledge the fact. She accompanied the others in search of sandwiches and coffee, laughing at Johnny's jokes, avoiding Cora's smug looks and completely ignoring Thad's thunderous frown.

The wind had picked up and the western sky had taken on a brassy look by the time they returned to the wharf, and after duly admiring the new acquisition, Cora, assisted by Thad, stepped down onto the Shearwater. Pam, as usual, was beside Zeb, and Thad cast off the bow, jumping lightly aboard as Johnny prepared to let go aft. Moving along the side until he was abreast where Lyle still stood on the dock, ostensibly admiring the lovely village, Thad held out his hand.

"Come on, Lyle, or you'll have to jump for it. Hurry!"

Zeb raced the engines and adjusted the throttle as Lyle called gaily over the noise, "I'm going with Johnny in the runabout. See you back at Hatteras!" She stepped back as Johnny let go the line and the Shearwater moved out slowly. As the gap widened between her and the furious Thad, Lyle thought with satisfaction, if looks could kill . . .

"Ready? Put that slicker back on, then. It's going to be wet."

"It'll be great! I'm going to love it!"

"Yeah, well, I ought to have my head examined for letting you come with me," Johnny grinned, settling her into the tiny cockpit. "Old Thad's going to curdle milk for a few days, but I have to go to Wanchese first thing tomorrow, fortunately, so I won't be around to catch hell."

"Maybe I'd better go with you," Lyle ventured, her bravado slipping away as the Shearwater turned to enter the channel and was lost to sight momentarily.

"What?" Johnny yelled over the sputtering roar.

"I said, maybe I should go with you!"

"No way! My Wanchese honey would kill me!"

"Fair weather friend!" she yelled, laughing excitedly as they skimmed out into the open sound.

Johnny simply had to show off his new possession and after they passed the more sedate Shearwater, they spun away, making wide circles that sent the spray flying out behind them in crystal rooster tails. As the wind picked up, the cold, salty water was blown back, so that by the time Lyle climbed dizzily out onto the wharf at Hatteras, some forty-five minutes or so later, she was drenched, despite the yellow slicker. Her hair was wet, there were runnels of icy water trickling down her back, and even her jeans were soaked. She was laughing helplessly, still exhilarated by the wildest ride she had ever had in her life, when she found herself face to face with a coldly furious Thad.

"If you're quite sure you've had enough for one day, Lyle, perhaps you'd be so good as to come along to the car," he said with deceptive calm.

Lyle's heart plummeted. "All right," she said meekly, allowing herself to be marched off to where Cora waited in the front seat of Thad's Mercedes. His grip, as he handed her in the back, was none too gentle.

No one spoke during the whole trip back up the beach to Frisco and as they neared the Knob, Lyle wriggled forward in anticipation of being dropped off.

Instead, Thad proceeded to his own house and pulled up on the marled driveway under the enormous live oak. He switched off the engine and tossed the keys once or twice as if undecided about something. Finally, when the atmosphere had thickened uncomfortably, both Thad and Cora spoke at once; she to declare that she was for settling down with the tallest of drinks, and Thad to outline his plan's for Lyle's immediate future.

Sitting miserably on the backseat, Lyle, herself, tried to keep her teeth from chattering, tried to ignore her sogginess, and tried to come to terms with the disconcerting feeling of being still at sea. Her stomach gave a peculiar roll and she thought for a dreadful moment she was going to be sick.

"Come on, then," Thad ordered, holding the door open for her. "Did you hear one word I said?"

Numbly, she shook her head, following miserably along behind the two of them. Once inside, she would have given anything to be allowed to flop on the floor in front of the banked coals in the fireplace. Instead, she found herself marched off to her bedroom, ordered in no uncertain terms to strip, and further admonished to make it snappy.

Thad, after issuing the succinct edict, strode to the bathroom where he turned on both faucets to the tub full blast. He returned immediately to find Lyle still standing where he had left her, and he commented dryly, "All this has a rather familiar ring, doesn't it?"

Lyle nodded. She had not spoken in so long, she wasn't sure her jaws were still functioning. They were clenched, as were her fists, but at the sight of the old mocking twist of Thad's lips, she relaxed somewhat. At least his eyes had lost that glacial quality, she thought thankfully.

"Get in the tub and soak until you thaw out. Meanwhile, I'll make some coffee."

"I don't think I want anything to drink, thanks," she managed weakly, still uncertain of her stomach's probable response to Thad's powerful brew.

"Nonsense! Coffee will settle your stomach and get you warmed up inside. Now hop to it!"

"How did you know about my—my stomach?" she wondered aloud, peeling off the damp cardigan she wore over Pam's turtleneck shirt.

"Your little fling last night set the stage, and it doesn't take much imagination, in view of that beet red nose and cheeks set in a pea green face, to figure out how you're feeling about now."

"Oh, Thad—," she began miserably, all the fight gone out of her.

"Never mind, honey. From the look in those eyes of yours you'd like to crawl in a hole and pull it in after you, but it's not so bad. You're allowed a few indiscretions in the process of growing up and I'd be willing to bet you haven't even started on your quota yet. Now, go get in the tub, Lyle, and I'll get your coffee going. Wrap up well when you get out, hmm?"

The water stung like fire and she told herself that she deserved it. Would she ever outgrow her rash nature? As the water cooled, her stomach eased and the burning on her face was all but forgotten until after she dried off and slathered lotion on her chapped skin. It was agony, and until a better penance came long, it would do very well, she told herself wryly.

In bed with the covers pulled up under her chin, she sipped sleepily on the over sweetened coffee Thad had left on her bedside table. His fury was dreadful but he could be so utterly, disarmingly, gentle—pity he would soon have no more reason to be either with her. Her usefulness would soon be at an end, surely, and he would break the engagement. If she had a ring, she might even hand it back to him unasked, beating him to the punch. That would be satisfying, she mused drowsily—her pride would be satisfied, at any rate.

"You decent?" Thad called through the door, and not waiting for an answer, he opened it and crossed swiftly to her bed. Missing nothing, he surveyed the slight form beneath the covers, taking in the fat braid lying across the pillow, the lobster pink face and the high collar of her flannel nightgown with its touch of lace.

"Hungry?" he asked.

"No. I'll be asleep before I even finish this coffee," she murmured, gazing at his shower fresh hair and the familiar three furrows on his brow. He looked tired, she thought unexpectedly, feeling her heart flop over in her chest.

"I could make you an omelet, the bachelor's stand-by."

"Hmmm, no thanks, Thad. I'll just have a nap, I think."

"You remind me of a baby bird I once rescued after it fell from the nest," he told her softly, adjusting the shade of her lamp so it did not shine in her face.

Too sleepy to dissemble, she replied, "They're not very pretty, are they?"

"No, not very," he agreed, with an unexpected warmth in his voice. He stared down at her a moment longer, then leaned down and kissed her lightly on the corner of her mouth. "Not pretty at all, little sweetheart. Go to sleep now. Cora and I will run over to the Knob to be sure Hesty's all right. 'Night."

Four days later Hesty had another attack. Lyle was with her at the time, for Mauncey had left early to look in on her granddaughter, who was recovering from chicken pox.

Pam was on hand, fortunately, and she managed to catch both Mauncey and the doctor in. Ethel had gone to pieces, for her strength had seemed to wane after Hesty's first attack, and Lyle, unable to leave the bedside, was driven almost to distraction by the sound of her wailing sobs.

She managed to get a pill under Hesty's tongue, praying all the time that Doc Titus would hurry, and when she heard Thad's deep, reassuring voice reach over Ethel's keening to bring it down to muffled sobs, she breathed a heartfelt, thank God!

By the time Titus left Hesty's room, dark had fallen and out on the Cape, seen through the blowing branches, was the pointing finger of light that could be seen all the way out to Diamond Shoals. Ethel had pulled herself together long enough to make a plate of sandwiches and gallons of coffee and both Zeb and Johnny stopped by to see if they could help.

Lyle's head was beginning to throb and she relaxed in a chair and extended her legs in front of her, letting her eyes close momentarily. The tension had been unbearable for the first few hours, but half an hour ago, Mauncey had stuck her head out the door to nod encouragingly and that had eased the pressure somewhat.

"Here, Lyle, you need this." Thad held out a thick sandwich and a mug of steaming coffee.

"Oh, Thad. I didn't hear you come in. I'm not sure I can get anything down. Did I doze?" She blinked uncertainly, gathering up the threads of the past few hours that had slipped from her mind for a few minutes.

"You weren't asleep long enough. Your lids dropped and then I barged into your rest with this. You need it, though. Ethel said you didn't have any lunch and I know for a fact that you didn't eat breakfast."

She took the mug and sandwich, only to put them down hurriedly when they heard the doctor's voice in the hall. She and Thad were on their feet instantly and two pairs of eyes turned anxiously toward the door.

"I'm sorry, Lyle—Thad. It's not going to be too long now. Matter of days, weeks, at best." He shook his head, running his hand through hair that already stood on end.

"But shouldn't she be in the hospital?" Lyle cried.

"No need. Not a thing they could do for her that would patch up a worn-out heart. Poor lady's been going strong for eighty-one years now, and she wants to end up in her own bed, her own house. Seems right to me." He searched their faces and then, sensing agreement, nodded his head once or twice. "Wants to see you, Thad. Word of caution—she hasn't got much starch left in her, so you can't have more than a few minutes, but she will have her own way. Got all upset when I told her you'd be by to see her tomorrow."

Thad was already out the door, leaving a sad, silent little group behind him.

He was back within five minutes, a strange expression on his face. Still, he said nothing until the doctor had gone, leaving strict instructions to send for him if there was the slightest change. Ethel had been sedated and Pam sat stoically outside Hesty's door, an unread book held limply in front of unseeing eyes.

"I've brought your things back, Lyle," Thad said. "Cora's gone—under the circumstances it seemed best."

"Oh," she said blankly. Cora gone. Somehow, it was anticlimatic. Everything was at that point. The numbness that crept over body and mind was pierced suddenly when Thad told her they were going to be married in three days time.

She bit her lip against a sudden stab of pain. "I do hope you'll both be very—," she began.

"No, Lyle. You and I are going to be married."

While she struggled to summon words, she watched the play of expressions across his usually enigmatic face. When she managed to ask him why, he replied simply that Hesty wished it.

Like someone awakening from a deep sleep, Lyle shook her head to clear it. "But Thad," she protested, "it's not real. I mean, we're not really engaged. I wanted to tell her so, but I just couldn't. She thought we'd had some sort of lovers' quarrel."

"A privilege reserved for lovers," he returned with a brief, sardonic twist of the lips. "As far as Hesty knows, we're engaged, and marriage is only a matter of time. Since she knows full well that time is not a commodity she can count on anymore, she wants us to marry as soon as possible in her own room, where she can see the deed done to her satisfaction. I more or less committed you, Lyle. I'm sorry if you think I did the wrong thing."

Lyle's sigh was compounded of a mixture of things, some of which would not bear scrutiny, but she admitted he had done the only thing possible under the circumstances.

They were married three days later in Hesty's room, with Zeb and Pam for attendants, Ethel weeping copiously, Hesty beaming fatuously and Mauncey managing the whole affair most capably. The doctor and Johnny had drinks ready in the living room afterward and everyone toasted the couple with surprisingly good champagne.

There had been only a few minutes before the wedding in which to wonder, for Lyle had been kept unusually busy every minute of the day. Thad had stayed away, whether by accident or design, and it was on the eve of the wedding that he sought her out to slip on her finger an exquisite ring of sapphires and diamonds.

"To match your eyes," he told her, brushing a kiss on the top of her head. He had been slightly distant for the past two days and Lyle had almost changed her mind a hundred times.

How could she possibly go through with it? The marriage would be a farce, just as their engagement had been, and that had been bad enough. But to live with him, to actually take his name as her own—could she do it? Would she be strong enough to maintain some semblance of independence so that if—not if, but when—the marriage was over, she could walk away without limping too badly?

Thad had told her they were marrying because Hesty wanted it and she was too ill to thwart. He had never indicated by word or deed that he wanted Lyle's love, wanted a real, lasting relationship with her.

What of those kisses? she asked herself, lying awake in the bed as the clock downstairs ticked away the last night of her single life. *He was a man, though, and a man did not have to be in love in order to make love, did he? Would he expect her to fulfill her role as his wife? Could she possibly do that and still bear to let him go when the reason for their marriage no longer existed?*

With a tortured cry, she rolled over and buried her face in her pillow. There were no answers to the question that battered her bewildered mind and it was growing light on the eastern horizon before she slept.

The impromptu reception was kept quiet and small, for Hesty's sake, and for that Lyle was thankful. She was ill at ease, even knowing she looked better than she had in ages in the apricot wool crepe that made the most of her small, but quite adequate curves. The rich pastel made her own color glow incandescently, and if she glowed a bit more colorfully whenever she looked at the tall, stern man in dark gray worsted, then no one seemed to think it out of the ordinary.

"I claim the prerogative of the best man," Zeb announced, emboldened by his third glass of champagne into dropping a kiss on one side of her nose. That started the movement and Doctor Titus, blushing furiously, kissed her loudly on the cheek and pumped Thad's hand enthusiastically. Johnny dusted off his hands and, declaring himself a better marksman than either of the others, proceeded to kiss her long and lingeringly on her mouth, to her acute embarrassment, and she struggled away, laughing.

"Dibs on you if he ever dumps you, hear?" he whispered loudly.

"If you're able to tear yourself away, Mrs. Creed, we'll be going." Thad said with a withering look at her.

Lyle looked up in surprise to see her new husband at her side. He had been standing somewhat apart from the rest of the group nursing a glass of champagne for several minutes, and she had not heard him approach.

"Going?" she asked wonderingly

"Did you expect to honeymoon at Durant's Knob?" His slightly chilly amusement sent Lyle's fragile poise toppling and she handed her glass to Ethel, murmuring something about getting her coat.

"Your bag is already in the car," Thad informed her as he draped her tweed coat over her shoulders and ushered her into the hall through a ragged spurt of good wishes.

"But—how did it get there?"

"Pam obliged."

"Where are we going?" She allowed herself to be seated in the car but she had to curb her impatience until he came around and seated himself behind the wheel.

"Thad, where are we going, and why?"

"We're going to Kitty Hawk, Mrs. Creed, because Hesty just might ask a few awkward questions if we stuck around as if there had been no ceremony at all."

"Oh, you mean—," she broke off in embarrassment, twisting her "something borrowed" handkerchief until it parted from its lace edging in several places.

"I mean if we were afraid to take off for even a short honeymoon, Hesty might get the idea her health is even more precarious than it is," he finished calmly.

"Oh," Lyle breathed, as understanding dawned. "I understand. Hesty might not understand a—a marriage of convenience," she said with all the composure she could summon.

Thad made no reply, but Lyle couldn't help but

notice the whitening of his knuckles as he downshifted with rather less finesse than usual.

Neither of them found much to say until they were well into the Nags Head area. They passed the motel where Lyle had stayed only weeks before and Thad asked casually, "Is that the place you spent Christmas?"

"Yes."

"Doesn't look particularly cozy."

"It wasn't. I—I preferred it that way, actually."

"No nosy strangers who might find a crack in that brittle wall you've built around yourself, is that it?"

"As a matter of fact, I wasn't only with strangers," she blurted out impulsively. "Cora was there, too. At least, I saw her one day and we had lunch together." She immediately regretted her lapse and her hands began twisting in her lap, this time working on the strap of her handbag.

"Cora Lambert? Just the two of you? Odd, you didn't mention it before."

"It wasn't odd. There was nothing to mention. We didn't have all that much to talk about. There was— another friend with us, as a matter of fact."

"Bill? Cora's husband?"

"Ex-husband, you mean."

"To be sure, ex-husband. They seem to come in several different catagories, don't they?"

"No, it was—someone else," she mumbled, wanting only to leave the uncomfortable topic. There was no real reason not to mention Stan, she told herself, nevertheless, Lyle was relieved when they pulled into the parking lot of one of the smaller, more exclusive hotels in the area.

"Pity it's not summer," Thad commented some

minutes later, as they walked about the suite of rooms he had engaged, "we could go swimming. What did you do when you were here Christmas?"

"Walked, mostly. It's nice when you have the beach to yourself."

"Will you mind sharing it this trip?" he asked with an odd little smile.

"Of course not," she hastened to assure him, turning away as she felt the hated color flood her face again. She had not been quick enough, for he laughed, and it was not a particularly kind laugh.

"Oh, well—you'll learn. You take this room," he continued briskly. "and I'll have the other. I'll give you half an hour to freshen up and then we'll go have some dinner, all right?"

She nodded tiredly, unable to lift her eyes for fear he'd see the tears that had inexplicably sprung into them. She was tired, that was all. It was only natural after weeks of nursing, plus the extra housework and all the tension of the past few days. By tomorrow, everything would fall back in place and she would be able to laugh at her bridal jitters. Thad would probably call it vapors, she thought wryly, remembering almost with affection the way he had teased her in the past for her dated expressions and mannerisms.

Thad's impeccable manners persisted throughout the evening. They dined superbly in beautiful surroundings and Lyle could not have remembered one item she ate half an hour later, nor could she recall the name of the restaurant. They danced for awhile and Thad held her as though she were the parson's grandmother. It was just after eleven when they returned to their suite and Thad asked her what she wanted to do the next day.

"Oh, walk, I suppose," she shrugged, finding it

impossible to conceal her overwhelming weariness. "I'm sorry," she apologized, stifling a yawn. "I don't know why I'm so sleepy."

"Get a good night's sleep, my dear. You'll find it easier to relax tomorrow." He hesitated and Lyle thought he was going to kiss her good-night, but he merely nodded and turned to his own room, closing the door firmly after him.

Over breakfast Thad, ruggedly attractive in jeans and a dark pullover, told Lyle he had called Titus last night and that Hesty was holding her own.

"Chances are she'll go on for some time like this, he now thinks. She seems to have passed a critical period and there's a good chance she'll make it a lot longer than he thought before. No improvement, of course, her poor old heart's worn out."

"Oh, Thad, it's so pitiful! Her eyes are so alive and you can see the impatience in them. She lies there wanting to get on with her affairs, hating it because she can't." She broke off, unable to control the tremor in her voice.

"Here, have some buttered toast," he offered, passing the pot of homemade fig preserves. "Keep your priorities in order, my dear. Hesty's lived out a longer term than a lot of folks do and she's been comparatively healthy up until a few weeks ago. She has her family with her, she's in her own home and she's not suffering. Under the circumstances, you can't ask for much more."

"It's the circumstances, themselves! Oh, I know, Thad, you're right, but all the same . . ."

"All the same, Lyle, you can't put back the clock, can you?" He leveled her a look that she found hard to understand.

The wind had dropped and the fog was rolling in across the ocean, much as it had done the last time Lyle had been on that particular stretch of shore. Thad took her arm as they climbed the dune and they stood there for several minutes, watching the sullenly heaving surf appear magically from beneath the trailing gray chiffon, hearing the raucous cries of the shore birds as disembodied plaints, and for no obvious reason, Lyle's spirits began to rise.

"I love the way it smells, don't you? I think I'll start walking a least a mile or two a day when we get back home. The idea of jogging never appealed to me. too much wasted energy, as if you should at least be charging a battery or something, but walking's different."

He laughed down at her, urging her on down the other side of the dune before dropping her hand. "Different in what way, other than the obvious."

"That depends on what the obvious is. To you, I mean."

"Speed, you silly child," he grinned.

"Oh. Well, there's that, of course, but sounds—when you're jogging, all you hear is puffing and panting, but when you're walking, you can hear your feet squeaking in the sand, and—and the frying sound the water makes when it curls up at the edges, and—and—"

"And the sounds of traffic and the barking dogs and the yelling children," he added with mock gravity. "Come on, let's try running here on the beach. Maybe you'll hear a new and different sound, unless you're just trying to excuse your laziness."

He struck out in a long, easy lope and it was all she could do to maintain her relative position. There was no way she could catch up to him until he slowed and steered her up to a protected hollow in the dunes.

They sprawled on the damp sand, watching a fleet of small trawlers working close inshore, and Thad told her about the pogie boats that fished for a trash fish used mostly in petfood and fertilizer.

"I've never heard of—pogies? Or is it porgies?"

"Porgie is a delicious fish, but the fish these men go after are called menhaden or mossbunkers or fatbacks. Don't ask me where the pogie came from but that's what the boats are called."

Lyle shivered with the penetrating damp and instantly, Thad was on his feet, pulling her up. She was throbbingly aware of his closeness and to cover her lack of ease, she made a business of brushing off the sand that clung to her clothes, meanwhile managing to put as much space as possible between them.

Silently, they strolled back toward the hotel. Lyle occasionally stooped to pick up a small shell or a tiny bit of driftwood and Thad, slowing his steps to match hers, stared out at the busy trawlers. An odd constraint had fallen between them and Lyle was not at all certain quite why.

At least, on Thad's part. If she, herself, were frequently ill at ease with him, it was all to easy to understand. After all, she was hopelessly, helplessly in love with the man and it was a refined sort of torture to find herself married to him.

The irony of the situation took her breath away as she considered it. A freak chain of events had brought about the untenable relationship and now she found herself constantly waiting for the other shoe to drop.

When would he go back to Cora? He had said he wanted to spare the feelings of her family by avoiding an open break, but what sort of sense did that make? Cora made no bones about the fact that she still considered him her property and she had been the one to leave him, not the other way around.

Would they wait until the marriage was ended or would they begin a discreet affair—perhaps a few business trips to Elizabeth City?

How could she bear it? She simply must, that was all. Her pride would not allow her to reveal how deeply her own feelings were involved, because heaven knew, if Thad ever discovered how utterly she melted at his touch, she'd have no barriers at all.

"What on earth is causing that astounding array of expressions to parade across your face?" he asked lazily. "If you were about three weeks old, it would be called gas, except by the doting parents who would insist it was a smile of recognition."

"Would you believe hunger?" she parried.

He caught up with her and placed a hand on each side of her waist and replied, "I'll believe it if you say so, but there's not much physical evidence that you exist on food at all."

His fingers bit into her tiny middle, then dropped to her hips. "Now here we find slightly more indication, but hardly enough to warrant more than one feeding a day." His hands moved deliberately up to cup her small breasts, an act that left her paralyzed and breathless. "Might conceivably require two meals a day to maintain these, but—" The silent laughter in his lazily provocative voice was more than enough to break through her momentary paralysis and she spun away, her feet kicking up sand as she flew toward the dubious sanctuary of the hotel.

He caught up with her in less than half a dozen

strides and ringed her wrist in a deceptively gentle manacle.

"Let me go!" she choked, face flaming beneath his cool amusement.

"What are you running from, Mrs. Creed?" he demanded softly.

"Don't call me that," she flashed, jerking her arm.

"You *are* that. Just what are you frightened of, anyway? Or should I ask, what *aren't* you frightened of?"

Outrage gave way to bewilderment. "What do you mean?"

"You're obviously afraid of me. You were afraid to admit your tender age and your relationship to Hesty and unless I'm very much mistaken, you're afraid of Cora Lambert."

"I am not!"

"Unless it's jealousy," he continued smoothly with a tantalizing quirk of one heavy, black brow.

She quickly sidestepped that particular pitfall. "That's ridiculous! I *did* tell Hesty who I was!"

"Finally."

"All right—finally," she admitted weakly.

"We'll skip the twenty going on thirty act and go on to the next subject—your husband. You still claim you're not afraid of me?" He towered over her for all her five feet seven inches and with the fog swirling about them, they might be the only two people in the world.

"Of course I'm not afraid," she lied belligerently. "We just—well, we simply have to come to some sort of understanding, that's all. There hasn't been any time to talk about our—our arrangements, everything has been so hectic lately."

"Maybe not hectic enough," he murmured enigmatically.

She looked at him suspiciously. It was often hard to tell when he was teasing and when he wasn't. "What do you mean?"

As if in answer to her hesitant question, he swung her easily against his body, closing his arms around her before she could push him away.

"No," she gasped, twisting her head away as he moved his face inexorably closer to her own. He grabbed her hair, twisting his fingers in it as he raised her face to meet his, and as his eyes darkened before her frightened gaze, he murmured, "Don't ever cut this marvelous, flaming mop, promise?"

Dimly, as though observing her own feelings from somewhere outside her body, Lyle was aware of the contrast between the chill, damp air that beaded moisture on Thad's sweater and the hot, firm sweetness of the mouth that explored her own in a sensuous assault that left her trembling uncontrollably. She was aware, with a strange sort of objectivity, of the fact that she was clinging to him helplessly, pressing her body shamelessly close to his as she caught fire from his own arousal.

The fog swirled thickly around them as Thad's hand moved to slide up her sweater, burning its way slowly to her breast to trace the hardening peak. His other hand trailed down her back, triggering off sensations she had never experienced before and when he caressed her hips, bringing that part of her anatomy into frightening closeness with his own demanding body, Lyle stiffened.

The cool air chilled her face as he lifted his own

to give her a look of inquiry from beneath heavy lids.

"No, Thad—please. There'll be none of that," she whispered hoarsely.

"You can't pretend you don't want me as much as I want you," he insisted, in a soft triumph ringing in his deep voice.

"I mean it. You promised, Thad—you did!"

"All I remember promising is to take you for better or for worse. To *take* you, my wife."

Stricken, Lyle pulled herself from his arms, covering her ears against the sure seduction of his words. "You know what I mean," she implored. "That was for Hesty's sake. It didn't mean anything, Thad—it didn't!" She was in quicksand and she knew it.

He stared at her, his face hard and impassive, then he shrugged. "No, it didn't mean anything," he agreed bleakly. "Put it down to proximity, that and the fact that we're supposed to be on our honeymoon." He laughed shortly, a sound that tore through Lyle's pitiful defenses, and he picked up a shell to hurl it out into the infinity of the mist.

She couldn't move. She simply stood there, waiting for something, and she didn't know what it was; she knew only the emptiness of her own aching heart.

"Look, Lyle, I'm no monk. I won't make any promises I can't be sure of keeping," Thad said when he turned to her, his shoulders hunched and his hands in the hip pocket of his jeans. "If it means so much to you to maintain your frosty little shell, I'll do my best to cooperate—up to a point," he qualified with a grim smile, "but you may have to put up with an occasional kiss, consider it your wifely duty."

"Temporary wife!" she flung at him defensively.

"That seems to be the most prevalent kind these days."

Was it bitterness, that alien note in his voice that roughened it to the point where Lyle almost relented? She felt the icy core inside her begin to thaw a little.

"Thad, it's not as if we cared for each other. Not that way, I mean." A unilateral love affair doesn't count, she told herself masochistically. "At least we can be friends, can't we? For Hesty's sake. It will make things so much easier."

"Will it?" It *was* bitterness. "I suppose you're right—for Hesty's sake. Rome wasn't built in a day, and even old Joshua wasn't the whiz he's commonly supposed to be."

They resumed walking slowly, each wrapped in private thoughts, and just before they crested the dune behind their hotel, Thad slowed and Lyle turned to him questioningly.

"Look, Lyle, I'm sorry if I've made things more difficult for you. Sometimes I get impatient, but—well, suffice it to say, it won't happen again. I eased off last night knowing you'd been hurt—we both have, I guess—but you've built up a pretty rigid barrier and I have no intention of bringing it down on your head."

"I know, Thad. I appreciate it. Men are—well, different, but I understand these things," she assured him sagely, bringing a welcome gleam of amusement to his face. Anything was better than the frozen misery she had glimpsed moments before.

"We both have a few problems to work out, my dear," he told her with amazing gentleness. "Shall we agree to be as kind to each other as possible under the circumstances? For Hesty's sake," he added almost as an afterthought.

It was all she could do not to throw herself back into his arms, but she simply nodded her agreement. Darn! How could she hold out against such tender understanding? If she weren't careful, he could undermine all her resolutions!

Chapter Eight

In the days that followed the brief honeymoon trip, Lyle sometimes imagined they were all players following a set script. Thad and she moved back into his house, maintaining a politeness that saw them through all but the most unexpected instances.

Hesty brought the color flooding to Lyle's face on more than one occasion with her weak, but ribald remarks, and Pam, dropping over one morning to get Thad's opinion on an idea for the renovation of the Knob, caught Lyle with her arms full of linens, headed for the guest room. She had done the laundry, had changed Thad's bed and was on her way to do her own.

"Who's coming to visit?" Pam asked curiously.

"Nobody that I know of," Lyle replied before she thought.

Thad, coming from his workroom at that moment, took in the situation at a glance and asked Pam blandly whose house she had come to inquire about, his or Hesty's.

"Well, Hesty's, actually. She wanted to know how I planned to change the upstairs, and—," she broke off with a puzzled look at Lyle.

"Come on in here, then, and let my bride get on with her spring cleaning." He turned Pam toward his workroom, leaving Lyle to her chores.

As she leaned against the bedroom door, limp with embarrassment, she heard Pam's voice clearly observing that it was a little early for spring cleaning.

"New broom," Thad remarked laconically. "Now, if it's about the northeast room, I've been checking on the price of roll insulation . . ."

Lyle heard no more, nor were there any more awkward questions about the allocation of sleeping quarters in the Creed household.

As fast as she could get through her morning chores, Lyle hurried to the Knob. She wanted to spend as much time as possible with Hesty, but it was also an excellent excuse to keep out of Thad's way. He worked several hours a day in the big, airy room where he had his drawing tables, filing cabinets, a desk and some odd storage units that held drawings. The room was businesslike, its walls painted a pale, warm gray and the large expanse of glass, facing north through the tall pines, was lightly covered with a natural, open weave linen. She felt oddly inclined to linger whenever she brought a tray of mid-morning coffee, but Thad maintained a cool politeness that discouraged familiarity as he thanked her and went back to his work.

Not that there was anything unfriendly in his treatment of her—it was simply impersonal, as if she were Berthalee, the absent housekeeper who seemed inclined to remain with her grandchildren indefinitely. Of course, that was exactly what she wanted from him—wasn't it?

Only at night, lying in her double bed listening to the impatient sounds of his pacing, the occasional slamming of a drawer or the rush of water from his shower, she wondered how it would all end. Would she ever again be able to get through a day or a night without seeing his broad, thick shoulders, his hair all tousled from running a hasty hand through it as he worked, or the quick, warm flash of his eyes as he passed her in the hall? This living together had its drawbacks when one of the partners was completely uninvolved and the other was a melting, aching void!

Over breakfast one morning when they had been married just over two weeks, Thad broached the subject of clothes.

"Look, I think it's about time you added to your wardrobe, Mrs. Creed, and I'd like to suggest a little color. You've been wearing that same dress now ever since we were married."

"Of course I haven't," she protested, passing him the dish of Berthalee's grape jelly.

"If it's not the same one, it might as well be, because they all look alike. You have gray and brown, gray and beige, gray and navy and gray again. You trying to maintain some sort of camouflage, or maybe to compensate for mother nature?"

"For your information I don't like flashy clothes."

"For your information I don't either, but even the pilgrims made a little progress."

"Clever. If you don't like the way I dress, you didn't have to marry me."

"I don't think we need to go into all that again, do you?"

"I guess not," she admitted grudgingly. "I'd better hurry. It's late and I want to get a load of laundry started before I go over to see Hesty."

"I think instead, we'll run up to Buxton. That's where you and Pam got that dress you were married in, isn't it? If they don't have anything to suit you, we'll go on to Nags Head."

"But Thad! You don't understand—"

"Money?" he asked, giving her a level look.

She flushed again and turned away, brushing the crumbs from the table in front of her. "I have some," she admitted, faltering slightly when she thought of how little she did have. The wedding dress had eaten a big hole in her meager reserves.

"That's not important. You're my wife and I'll support you. Come on, do what has to be done and let's go. Now that I think about it, I'm really looking forward to seeing you in something that looks as if it were designed in this century."

"Look, I told you once—!"

"Calm down, firecracker. I haven't forgotten anything you ever told me. Just remember, though, I'm the one who has to sit across the table from you three times a day. I think I'd enjoy a more cheerful view for a change." He was teasing, she knew he was, for the familiar gleam was evident, but it did hurt, all the same.

Silently, she cleared away the breakfast things, put the washing on and shrugged into her coat, not even bothering to look in the mirror. If her looks were all that hopeless, what did it matter, anyway? She picked up her purse and went into the living room, sitting on the edge of her chair to stare dolefully out the window.

It was fully ten minutes when she heard the soft

exclamation behind her. "Well—how long have you been moping here? Why didn't you tell me you were ready?"

"It's your trip. I figured we'd go when you were ready," she shrugged.

Thad crossed the room in easy strides to stand before her. "Ah, Lyle, I'm making a botch of it, aren't I? Honey you know it doesn't matter to me if you want to wear flour sacks. I just want to see you happy, that's all. I've been doing my best to go easy on you, but sometimes I get impatient."

"Oh, I know, Thad, I'm sorry too. You said you had problems to work out and I don't help matters by getting all sulky, do I?"

"Not sulky. Prickly would be more like it," he grinned.

"Well, prickly then," she conceded. "I'll try to do better, but about the clothes—is it really all that important to you?"

"Yes, it's really all that important to me," he mocked gently. "You flicker around here like a painfully shy little ghost, trying to stay out of my way, and it makes me nervous. I think I'd prefer it if you stormed and stomped around, maybe sang a little at your work, and for Pete's sake, wear something with some color to it!"

Her laugh bubbled over. "I'll go along with the storming and the stomping, but if you'd ever heard me sing, you'd retract that request."

"Consider it retracted. And the colors?"

"You're calling the shots, Mr. Creed. Anything but cerise. It makes me look like a piece of pop art."

"I'm not at all certain I'd recognize cerise if I met her face to face," he observed facetiously.

They went to Nags Head, where Thad spent far more

money on her than Lyle thought he should, but he seemed determined to make her enjoy herself and she found it all too easy to succumb to his charm. She protested that she'd never have an occasion to wear the two evening dresses he insisted on seeing her in, a brown lace with a jacket and an oyster satin cut along deceptively simple lines. In the end, of course, she gave in, taking them both because he wouldn't have it any other way.

It was too late for lunch by the time they left the shop and Lyle confessed to being famished. Thad solved their dilemma by taking her to a delicatessen, where he bought loads of rich foods, a handsome basket to carry them in, and a bottle of red wine to wash them down with. They drove to Pea Island wildlife reserve and ended up eating in the car when it began to drizzle.

"Oh, it's too much," Lyle laughingly protested when Thad urged another smoked salmon sandwich on her. "Do you realize I've already outgrown everything we just bought?"

Thad's eyes covered her lean figure in the brand new black watch plaid slacks and the bottle green mohair sweater. "Do *you* realize you've laughed more today than you have in all the time I've known you?" he asked quietly.

She turned to him slowly, gravity replacing the lingering smile as she stared at him with oddly stricken eyes.

"Lyle, what is it?"

Brushing the crumbs from her lap, she deliberately folded her napkin and thrust it into the basket, reaching into the backseat for her jacket. "I think we'd better be going, don't you? I didn't mean to be gone all day," she said anxiously.

"Stop it!" He removed the purse from her fingers and turned her to face him. "Now you listen here, I don't know what I said to make you come on like a tragedy queen, but nothing's changed in the past few minutes that I know of. You were happy enough until I brought it to your attention, so what is it?" He grabbed her shoulder and shook her, a look of baffled anger on his face.

How could she tell him? She couldn't put into words her sudden realization of what the rest of her life would be like after he no longer needed her. He had a way of creeping so insidiously into her heart, under her defenses—sometimes she could almost convince herself he had married her because he wanted to and not just for Hesty's sake.

"Do you hurt? Are you ill?"

"No, I'm not ill! Just—why can't you leave me alone? We were doing just fine until you got this thing about my clothes. What difference does it make, anyway? It can't last forever!"

"Nothing lasts forever, does it?" he asked bitterly, turning away to switch on the ignition. They headed south with Thad's foot so heavy on the accelerator that it drained the color from Lyle's face. She stiffened in her seat, staring straight ahead as he raced down the highway, the sparsely grassed dunes on the ocean side and the low lying marshes a blur on the soundside. Even in the fading light she was aware of the harshly forbidding set of his jaw.

Fortunately, there was little traffic, and gradually he eased off. "Sorry." He bit off the word and spat it out. Then, in a gentler tone, "I really am sorry, Lyle. I know you get frightened sometimes when someone gets too close to you, threatens to get under your guard, but

I thought we were better friends than that, or did something I say upset you?"

Some of the tension drained from her, leaving her tired and limp. "It's my own foolishness, Thad. I told you once I was a complete washout in polite society. You're such good company I forgot for a minute how temporary our relationship is."

"And that bothered you? You want something more?" The strange, intense note in his voice alarmed her and she withdrew into silence, afraid she had inadvertently revealed more than was wise.

After awhile, when the silence became uncomfortable, she filled it. "We both knew what we were doing when we got married, Thad. You knew what you were doing when we got engaged, I suppose, even if I didn't quite understand, but that's not important now, I guess. The thing is, nothing's changed since then. I don't expect you to go into any long-winded explanations, it's really none of my business, but I just want you to know you can trust me to go on with it as long—well, as long as there's any need."

She broke off nervously, her hands twisting on the handle of her pocketbook, and cast him a sidelong glance. He met it with one of his own, a baffling, enigmatic gleam of hazel eyes in the gold of the setting sun. Then, with a slight shake of his head, he directed his attention toward the road as they curved into Buxton Woods and picked up the traffic emerging from the lighthouse road.

"I don't know exactly what that slightly incoherent little speech meant, but we'll leave it alone for now," he said, and after that, neither of them spoke.

Lyle directed her attention toward the last gleam of sunlight over the Sound as they passed a schoolhouse, then Paradise Bay, Brigand's Bay and Indiantown Shores. The armed neutrality was assiduously maintained as Thad pulled up in front of the house and helped her bring in the various boxes and bags.

For the next few days, Lyle was almost shy as she dressed in her new finery. Thad made no comment, although she found his eyes on her more than once as she went about her work in the house. She wondered if he were picturing someone else in her place one night as he stared more intently than usual at her. She had made an effort with her hair and put on one of her prettiest new dresses, a deep wood-violet wool thing that made the most of her coloring as well as her figure.

"I have to go to Elizabeth City for a day or so," he announced over dessert, "and you're welcome to go along if you'd like."

Her heart leaped, then plummeted again. "I don't think so," she said, "I'd much rather stay home." It was one thing to deal with the knowledge of Cora from a distance, another to see them together.

"I don't want to force you to do anything you don't want to do, Lyle, but I wish you'd change your mind," he said at last.

"You really don't need me, Thad. I'd only be in the way with—well— Please don't make it more difficult for me. We've been getting along so well, lately, and I'd like to see us finish up with no hard feelings."

The color slowly drained from his face as he continued to stare at her, making him look years older. "Just what do you think this trip is all about, anyway?" he asked stiffly.

Shaken with a bewildering variety of emotions, Lyle could only shake her head dumbly. "Please, Thad, I've got a splitting headache and I just don't feel like arguing with you. I don't *want* to go with you. Isn't that enough? I'd much rather stay here alone."

The change of expression on his face was not a nice thing to see and Lyle stepped back instinctively.

"Alone? Or maybe Johnny has another boat trip planned for the two of you. I'm surprised he hasn't been around since our wedding, considering the splendid send-off he gave you. What was it he said? Dibs on you if I ever dumped you?" He had never sounded so hard and bitter, for all the anger she so often aroused in him, and Lyle withdrew behind her fragile barrier.

"All right, have your fun! I might have known a silly schoolgirl like you would be ripe for any fast talking, good-looking kid who paid you the slightest attention, but you could at least have waited until . . ." He broke off with an expletive, his eyes blazing.

Lyle swallowed painfully and tried to speak past the dryness in her mouth. "Thad, it's not what you think. Johnny—" Johnny meant nothing to her other than someone to laugh and joke with, someone undemanding who knew how she felt about Thad, but she couldn't tell him that. As they glared at each other, Lyle's indignation grew. How could he ask it of her, that she accompany him to see the woman he loved, the woman for whom he would soon be leaving her?

"Damn it, I'm not going, and that's that!" she exploded, stung beyond endurance by his unfeeling cruelty.

"In that case, Mrs. Creed, I might as well say good-bye right now! That way, I won't have to drag you out of your nice warm bed early in the morning."

Before her muscles could respond to the alarm, he was there, drawing her roughly, bruisingly into his arms. His hands tangled in her hair, pulling out pins, raking through the tumbling coils as his rough jaw scraped against the tender flesh of her throat.

"My God, I ought to—" he broke off, smothering her mouth with a kiss that brought her figuratively to her knees. She was reeling dizzily when he finally lifted his head and the eyes that stared down so intensely into her own were black with emotion, with anger, she thought, shrinking away from him.

"Sometimes I dream about this—" The words were wrung from him as he twisted his hands in her hair. The hands slipped to her shoulders, gripping with a fierceness that was almost as wounding as his anger, and he whispered, "Lyle, Lyle, what have I done to us—I promised I'd wait, but—"

Sensing his uncertainty, she pulled away, frightened by the overwhelming emotional war that raged within her, but oddly enough, no longer frightened by her husband. Something about him wrung pity from her aching heart and she reassured him in a trembling voice. "It will be all right, Thad. It will, you'll see. It's only that we were forced into something—something that neither of us wanted—" The lie was torn from her in an effort to assuage her own tattered pride. "But it will work out. Nothing's really changed, you know." Her breath was coming easier now, and she finished in a rush before she could give in to the terrible desire to weep her eyes out. "It's hard to keep things on a platonic basis when we're living together. You're a man and—and I'm a woman and these things happen, but don't worry, Thad—I haven't misunderstood anything."

He stared at her, his eyes blazing with a strange expression that completely baffled her. As he raised a hand, as if to touch her cheek, the phone rang stridently from the hall table and with a look of angry frustration, he turned away to answer it.

"It's for you," he said evenly, moments later. She had to brush against him to pass through the door and she could almost feel the waves of animosity emanating from his rigid body.

Her voice shook as she picked up the receiver and spoke into it.

"Lyle," Johnny's voice rang out clearly, "remember that Wanchese honey I told you about? Well, she's coming down with her brother just for the day tomorrow, and I thought you might like to meet her."

Lyle's head reeled, trying to throw off the holocaust of emotions that had swept over her within the past few minutes. "Wanchese honey?" she stalled, dimly remembering something she had heard not too long ago.

"Sure! Her name's Cecie Ballance, she's a schoolteacher. Look, I thought, if it's all right with you, the four of us could have lunch somewhere, then, you might be a doll and take the brother off my hands and give us a clear shot, what say?"

"But—" She had been going to say, why me? But here was the perfect opportunity to make Thad believe she was completely indifferent to his actions. She accepted the date for lunch, hearing, just after she did so, the slam of Thad's bedroom door.

"Good," she whispered aloud, returning slowly to her own room after hanging up the receiver. Won the battle, lost the war.

Lyle was certain she would not see Thad again before he left. In fact, to be sure she didn't, she remained in bed long past her usual hour for rising. Let him fix his own breakfast. He had done so often enough, she gathered, when Berthalee was off on one of her many jaunts. It was time that woman was returning, anyway. Maybe Lyle had done too much to make him comfortable, maybe he was just spoiled, taking advantage of a free housekeeper.

Not exactly free, she conceded, fingering the sheer nylon gown that was a small part of the clothes he had bought for her at Nags Head.

There was a light tap on the door and she looked up, startled to see Thad peering diffidently around it. "May I come in for a minute?" he asked.

She nodded, unable to speak.

"I wanted to give you a number where you could reach me in case you need to. A couple of numbers, in fact. If you can't get me one place, you can leave a message at the other." He placed a slip of paper on her bedside table, not taking his eyes from her as he spoke.

Instinctively, Lyle drew the covers up to her chin, but only after she noticed his straying glance. Old flannel was one thing; sheer nylon quite another. She did not know what had prompted her to buy it in the first place, much less to put it on last night! That was just one more of the silly, inexplicable things she had found herself doing in recent weeks.

"Are you certain you won't change your mind?" he asked, then, without waiting for an answer, "No, I forgot, you have plans today, don't you?"

She could not understand the sudden bleakness that emptied his eyes of all expression. "You—you don't really need me, do you? I mean, surely not at this stage?" Whatever arrangements he made with Cora now, nothing would be implemented until Hesty was no longer here to care.

"Why would I need you?" he asked coolly. "I just thought you might enjoy a break from all the housework you seem to have fallen heir to, here and at the Knob. Believe me, Lyle, when I married you, I had no intention for you to sub for Berthalee indefinitely."

"I know that," she exclaimed reassuringly, impulsively reaching out to touch his hand. "I don't mind in the least. It's nice—nice to be needed, for a change."

He leaned over swiftly and kissed her, straightened and was beside the door before she could recover. "Don't overdo it, my dear. I'll be back as soon as I can."

After he had gone, leaving an unbelievable amount of emptiness behind, Lyle lay there wondering at the very contagion of the man. His temper could ignite hers in a split second, but his tenderness could melt her deepest anger. His passion? Oh, Lyle, it's better not to dwell on that, she chided herself.

Perhaps she was being foolish to allow her pride to deprive her of a chance to experience love with a man. Thad had shown himself willing—the natural physiological reaction of any man living in close contact with a woman, she supposed. Could she? Did she dare let herself go, forgetting that in a little while it would be over and she would be left with the bitter dregs, if not an even more tangible reminder of her love?

And where is your fine wall now? What happened to your firm declaration of independence? she asked herself. But that was before she met Thad, before she had the cataclysmic misfortune to fall in love with a man who belonged to someone else.

It seemed only natural for Lyle to stay at the Knob. Thad had not said how long he would be away, but as he had taken a bag, Lyle assumed it would be at least overnight. She slept in her old damp, drafty room and lay awake far longer than was good for her, for her thoughts were filled with Thad and Cora and in spite of the stiffest admonitions to herself, she kept picturing them close together—as close as Lyle wanted so desperately to be to the man who was legally her husband.

Sometime during the night, she awakened to hear whisperings and stirrings. At first, she thought she was back at Thad's house, hearing the restless movements from his room across the hall, but at the familiar creak of the stairway, she realized where she was and swung out of bed.

Apprehension wrapped around her like a damp shroud as she went through the downstairs hall to the back room where Hesty had been ever since the first attack. Before she got as far as the kitchen she heard Ethel's quivering voice and Pam's stern rejoinder.

"What is it?" she whispered, approaching the bath-robe-clad figures.

"She's not good," Pam told her flatly.

"Have you sent for—no, of course you haven't. Look, I'll run home and call Doc Titus, all right?"

She ran through the darkness, trying to stiffen her face against the strong tendency to crumble, and only as she was hurrying back did she notice the streak of cold light that had touched the eastern horizon. Awakening, as she had, in the middle of the night, she had no idea of how near or far it was from daylight, not that even the strongest of suns could warm away this awful feeling of dread.

Hesty died just before noon. After hearing her painfully labored breathing and seeing the lively spirit reduced to a pathetic shell in a matter of a few hours, Lyle could not regret her passing. She wept inwardly, but it was for herself and the fact that she had lived so much of her life without even knowing her great-aunt—not for Hesty, who was at peace.

"Has anybody called Thad?" Pam asked, finding Lyle alone in her bedroom, where she had gone to escape the sympathetic neighbors who came as soon as the news got out.

"I guess not. I ought to call, but there hasn't been time to think."

Letting herself quietly out the back door, Lyle walked along the fragrant pine-straw-covered trail. It was cold and she had forgotten her coat but there was something revitalizing about the air, its very pungency, the smell of fecund earth, of rotting vegetation and dried weeds was a subtle reminder of the force of life that only awaited the passing of winter to burgeon forth again.

The slip of paper was still on her bedside table and she read the two numbers, wondering which to try first. He had given her no indication of whose they were. On impulse she dialed the last one first and listened to the impersonal ring on the other end. After three rings it was answered.

"Hello," came the disembodied voice, its familiar tones sending Lyle's sore heart plummeting.

"Cora, is Thad there? This is Lyle."

There was a small silence into which Lyle's nerves screamed in protest.

"He just left a few minutes ago, Lyle. You should have called earlier—or last night. We were in all night if you needed us. Was it anything important?"

Gathering all her resources, Lyle spoke evenly. "I'm afraid it is. Do you know where I can reach him?"

"He should be there within a few hours. He wanted to stay longer, but with Hesty so uncertain, he didn't dare. We'll just have to make it up another time." Then Cora's voice changed as she added threateningly, "You know, don't you, that I'm going to have him back? They say a man never forgets his first love and Thad and I grew up next door to each other. I was his first love, Lyle, and I'll be his last."

Unable to speak, Lyle simply hung up the phone. She stood there staring at the wall, seeing the woman who had just shattered her hopes.

Hopes! What hopes? Unconsciously, she clenched her fists, pressing them against her thighs. There was no hope, nor had there ever been. Thad had been perfectly honest from the beginning, even if he had been too chivalrous to put it into words. Cora had hurt him terribly, and before he could allow her to walk into his life again as if nothing had ever happened, he was compelled to make her suffer just a fraction of what he must have felt. From there on, the mock engagement had gotten out of hand and they had found themselves trapped in this pitiful farce. It was only now, hearing Cora admit that Thad had spent the night with her, and that he hated to return to his wife, that Lyle admitted to herself that in spite of everything, she had begun to hope.

It was just after four when Thad got home. Lyle had left a note for him in case he went on to his own place first, but seeing all the cars outside the Knob, he guessed.

During the next two days, there was not a single minute to speak of private matters. Medwin and Pauline came, as well as Ethel's sister from Hyde County, and they all had to be housed and fed, although the neighbors brought enough food for a siege. That, in itself, meant a constant stream of visitors, day and night, and by the time Lyle and Thad escaped to their own home each evening, they were both too exhausted to do more than fall asleep.

Lyle found it difficult to believe that Medwin was her cousin. He was a blustering little man, completely under the thumb of his socially ambitious wife, but on one of the few occasions when she talked to him without Pauline, she found him quite a different person.

Pam, Lyle and Medwin were seated around the kitchen table having coffee and Pam said, "Well, I guess you two timed things about right, Lyle." Medwin had asked about Cora. "I was afraid for awhile that that old harpy was going to snaffle him all over again."

"Pamela," Medwin exclaimed in faintly shocked tones, "I really don't think Lyle cares to have her marriage discussed this way."

"Oh, she doesn't mind. Lyle doesn't like Cora any better than I do, and anyway, I might have known that Thad would be twice shy after being once burned. At least Hesty got her wish."

"What wish? Oh, you mean that old thing about the two families." Medwin's smile indicated that he wasn't unfamiliar with Hesty's idea of uniting the Creeds and the Durants. He turned to Lyle and asked, "Did anything come to light about an old romance between Hesty and a Creed? I've been thinking, maybe she had a crush on one of Thad's ancestors and that's why she kept wanting to marry him to Pam—or to you. Sort of a vicarious thrill."

Before anyone could answer, Thad spoke from the doorway. No one had heard him approach. "I can't imagine Hesty's ever having anything so minor as a crush. If she had anything at all, it would have been a grand, flaming passion. She wasn't a timid woman and I'd lay odds she was a real beauty when she was younger. I'd like to think my grandfather had a fling or two before he married my grandmother. She was a pretty grim lady at best, but if they did, Hesty and granddad, I mean, I never heard of it."

Pam spoke up, "You wouldn't have heard anything, silly. Your grandpaw would have kept his trap shut if your grandmaw was all that grim and Hesty surely wouldn't have let on, not if it was a one-sided affair. No woman would ever admit to having loved in vain, as the saying goes, right, Lyle?"

For once, the sounds of the women's voices as they approached the kitchen to retrieve their dishes was a welcome break. For the life of her, Lyle could not have come up with an answer to Pam's teasing question.

Chapter Nine

For two weeks after the funeral, both Thad and Lyle avoided any mention of their future plans by silent mutual consent. It was too soon and they both found more to do than either of them expected. There was the estate, an uncomplicated matter, but time-consuming. Pam, as the prime beneficiary, received Durant's Knob, of course, and Ethel was left any money available. Lyle, to her complete surprise, inherited a small, but exquisite strand of pearls that no one even knew Hesty had owned.

Ethel was determined to clean the Knob from top to bottom before she moved in with her sister on the mainland and Pam and Lyle pitched in to help her. Dropping wearily into bed each night, Lyle wondered more than once why she worked to the point of exhaustion, for Ethel and Pam could have managed without her. She was forced to admit that it was only a means of keeping her mind occupied during the day and insuring a reasonably sound sleep at night.

Of Thad she saw surprisingly little. He seemed to be

on the home stretch of some large project that kept him closed up in his study till all hours. They met only at mealtimes and sometimes not even then.

The day after Ethel left, the Knob was closed while Pam and Zeb went to South Mills on a lumber buying trip. Lyle wandered restlessly about the house, wiping nonexistent dust from polished surfaces until lunchtime, when Thad emerged from his study to join her at the table.

Ignoring his soup, he stared at her for so long that Lyle made a quick, nervous movement that almost toppled her glass. "You know, you look awful," he said after awhile.

Her eyebrows flew up in pained surprise. "Well, I've never claimed—," she began.

"Oh, I don't mean *awful* awful. I mean you've been overdoing it. Here, let me see your hands." He reached across the table and took her hands in his, turning the palms up to expose the reddened skin and the newly formed callouses. "It's time for a break, honey. I can't have you falling apart on me now, of all times. Look—well, no, eat your soup first, and we'll take coffee in the living room afterward. There's something I want to talk over with you."

She could hardly force herself to spoon up the fragrant lime soup, but she knew Thad would have something to say if he thought she were starving herself. Most all of his personal observations during the past two weeks had had to do with the amount of food, rest or sleep she was getting.

"All right," she said, after bracing herself later on in the living room. "What did you have to tell me?"

"It's not so much a matter of telling you as of asking your cooperation. You see, I have to go to Elizabeth

City next Thursday, actually, sooner would be better but I can't make it until Thursday. Here, have some more coffee."

She could have screamed at him. Every nerve in her body was crying out against what he was proposing, even while a small, inner voice was calling her all sorts of a fool for not preparing herself for this eventuality—this inevitability!

"Where do I come in? Do you need me at this stage?"

"At this—well, of course I need you. It's the culmination of the whole shebang, the thing I've been working on night and day for the past six weeks or longer."

"Oh," she said in a tiny voice. "Well, of course I'm ready to cooperate in whatever way I can. You'll have to tell me what I'm supposed to do. I've never done this sort of thing before."

"Oh, for crying out loud, Lyle, there's nothing to it! You claim to have been some sort of social disaster when you were growing up, but you're a big girl now. Besides, you've grown up far more than you realize during the past few weeks. You've held things together, in fact. This is going to be a breeze and anyway, nothing will be required of you except your presence. You won't find it hard to be pleasant to the folks you'll be meeting, they're first-class. They'll love you, girl, so don't worry about a thing. I'll be right there with you and if you're feeling nervous, just kick me under the table and I'll distract everybody while you make a break for it."

Bewildered, she sat there holding a rapidly cooling cup of coffee and stared at him. As she slowly put the cup down on the edge of a book, Thad made a dive for it.

"What is it?" he exclaimed. "You're looking white as a sheet! Damn it, woman, no one can be that frightened of a little banquet for not more than fifty people. You're not meeting the First Lady, you know—she sent her regrets."

"A banquet! Thad, what are you talking about?" her voice broke on an upward note.

"Well, what the hell do you think I'm talking about? The dedication ceremony, groundbreaking, banquet and all the rest of the folderol that goes with launching any public project paid for with taxpayers' money. What did you think I meant?"

She gulped, wishing she could sink out of sight in one of the enormous, down-filled cushions on the sofa. "I—I thought you were starting the—the annulment proceedings," she said faintly.

"Annulment proceedings! What on earth gave you that idea?"

"Well, there's nothing to keep you from it anymore."

"Oh, hell!" He leaned his head on his fist, looking down at his big, bench-made moccasins. Then, raising his head again, he said firmly, "Look, leave any annulment business to me, will you? There's hardly been time to think about anything like that with this Sunset Towers project pressuring me. Can you be patient a little longer? I know we agreed, but you see, the thing is—well, I told the Simpsons about you and naturally they're expecting you to accompany me to all the festivities. It wouldn't matter so much but Luke Simpson was a special friend of my dad's and he's been close to me for as long as I can remember. He's chairman of the planning committee, you see, spear-headed the whole project, although that's not the reason I was chosen as architect, believe it or not." He grinned ruefully and Lyle's mind raced to catch up with enough details so she could piece together the whole story.

Thad had assumed she knew about the project he was working on. It was entirely possible he had mentioned it to her in the past, for she couldn't always account for the way her mind took off on its own tangent when they were together. Often she found her own fantasies more acceptable then the everyday realities.

"So you see," he continued, proving her suspicions about her own powers of concentration, "I've got to be there, as architect, and you, as my wife, have to be with me. It's a pretty staid bunch, as you can imagine, but they're not dull, by any means. You'll enjoy it, and I promise you, no creamed chicken and frozen peas."

Despite her prejudice against Cora's hometown, Lyle was delighted with her first glimpse of it. As they crossed the Pasquotank River bridge Thad pointed across the broad, dark water, lined with picturesque cypresses, to a shoreline that included boatworks, sporting many a tall mast, and a variety of handsome homes whose green velvet lawns sloped to the water's edge. There was an air of sleepy gentility that was immensely appealing to the senses, and even the knowledge that somewhere within its boundaries lived Cora Lambert could not mar the pleasure in her day.

They had stopped at Point Harbor for lunch and again at Grandy to admire an enormous hog farm, which Lyle declared must be called El Rancho Grandy.

Thad had announced in sonorous tones the towns of Spot and Mamie as they passed through and Lyle had insisted on leaving the highway to locate Waterlily, simply because she was entranced with its name.

It had come as something of a surprise to learn that they were to stay with Luke Simpson and his sister, Evelyn, but Lyle took it in stride until Evelyn showed them the lovely room that was to be theirs.

By the time they were left alone in the bedroom, Lyle's high spirits had disappeared entirely and she was firmly ensconced behind her wall again. "Just what did you mean by planning this?" she demanded furiously as soon as their hostess had gone. She gestured wildly at the room, dominated over by an enormous double bed.

"Climb down, Lyle. There was nothing deliberate about it, I can assure you." He took off his topcoat and hung it up, returning to relieve Lyle of hers.

"I'm not sleeping here with you, Thaddeus Creed, so you can just make other arrangements."

"Don't be paranoid," Thad retorted coldly. "I can assure you that I have no designs on your virtue. Sleep on that thing if you don't want to sleep in the bed." He gestured to the hard looking chaise lounge, "I don't give a damn."

"Why should I be the one to suffer and let you sleep in comfort? You're the one who arranged the trip. You can be the one to suffer if the accommodations aren't suitable!" she flung at him.

Thad gripped her arms until she flinched, his eyes blazing into hers with a frightening intensity. "We won't go into that now! The Simpsons are waiting downstairs and we'll join them in five minutes and there won't be one look or word to make them uncomfortable, is that clear? If my friends bore you, you can claim a headache and leave early and I can promise you that you won't be disturbed, no matter where you decide to sleep! Will that do for now?" His sarcasm ate into her like acid and she rubbed her aching arms when he flung her away from him. He looked suddenly defeated.

"I'm sorry, Thad. My darned temper again. I know you didn't do it on purpose—after all, they think we're married." Her anger had drained away, leaving an emptiness inside her.

"We *are* married, Lyle," he reminded her tersely.

Afterward Lyle remembered the evening as a montage of impressions: mahogany; gleaming silver and china; sparkling Waterford; rich, delectable food; and soft, drawling voices speaking with gentle courtesy. She had been caught up in spite of herself in the hospitality of the Simpson household.

Conversation centered mainly on the Sunset Towers project and she could only conclude that modesty on Thad's part had kept him from telling her how important it was. Luke Simpson was extravagant in his praise of the many ingenious innovations that would provide comfort, privacy and protection as well as room for individuality for the fortunate elderly people who lived there. Hopefully, it would be a prototype for more to come.

Lyle went upstairs first and she was climbing out of the tub when she heard Thad enter the adjoining bedroom. She slipped on her flannel nightgown—she had not worn the nylon again, and wished she had brought a bathrobe with her.

Thad had tossed his jacket across the chair and his shirt was unbottoned to the waist, revealing a thatch of body hair that glinted in the light of the brass chandelier. He flicked a derisive glance at her nightgown, his eyes dropping to her bare toes and rising slowly back up past the gentle swell of her breasts, past the high buttoned collar, to the throat and face that were warming with a blush of color.

She turned away, unnerved by the sight of his brawny, masculine chest and she heard his low, mocking laughter behind her. When she snatched the eiderdown from the foot of the bed and moved toward the chaise, he was beside her in an instant.

"Forget it. You're sleeping in the bed," he said softly.

"You can't sleep on that thing, you'll break your back."

"I have no intention of breaking my back, thank you." He removed the satin-covered quilt from her hands and tossed it behind him. It struck the edge of the bed and slithered onto the floor and neither of them moved to retrieve it. They were locked in a silent battle of wills, mocking hazel eyes holding apprehensive blue ones in thrall. Just when she could bear it no longer, he broke the tension.

"Have you seen the view from our window?"

"What?" She couldn't keep up with the lightning change of pace.

"Come over here." He took her unresisting hand and led her to the large, organdy-draped window that overlooked the river. The lights from the downtown section and the bridge across the way reflected like handfuls of diamonds cast carelessly across the black waters.

After several moments of tense silence, Lyle shivered and immmediately Thad's arm tightened about her shoulder. He turned her away from the window and they were back where they had been before; facing the double bed.

"Look, the bed is wide enough so that you don't face contamination. You stay on your side and I promise you, I'll stay on mine."

When Lyle opened her mouth to protest, he put a finger across her lips. "Don't say it, Lyle. Just don't say it. It's been one long grind, these past few months on this project, and I want to see an end to it with no more hassles. Tomorrow's going to be flack and static from the word go and I'd just like to get one decent night's sleep before we face the mob." He had led her around to the far side of the bed as he spoke and turned down the covers. When she slid between the cold linen sheets, he moved to the other side without so much as a glance at her.

"What mob? What kind of flack and static?" she asked as he climbed beneath the covers on the other side.

"A mob of contractors, bureaucrats, reporters all wanting to know why so-and-so got the contract for such and such and who decrees who'll be granted space in the project—why somebody's name was left off the guest list for the official opening ceremonies and when will the next project commence because they just happen to have a tract of land that would be ideal. Government money, taxpayers' money actually—it brings them all out of the woodwork."

From the other side of the bed, Lyle could feel the heat of his body and she edged slightly closer to the edge of the mattress. "But you were just the architect. Why are you mixed up in it?"

"Thanks," he laughed wryly. "But the whole thing means a lot to me and I'm involved right up to the finish line. If it should lead to more of the same, I want to see that the standards are maintained. No cheap copies of a damned good prototype. Now, if you don't mind, I'd like to catch a few winks before midnight. Luke and I have a breakfast appointment."

He turned his back on her and within minutes, she heard his breathing slow to a regular rhythm. Her own remained light and uneven for a good deal longer as she felt his nearness with every cell in her body.

Her last conscious thought was that somewhere in the city, Cora Lambert was sleeping and she couldn't help but feel a small, secret delight that for tonight, at least, Thad was in her own bed.

She struggled awake from a confusing, vaguely threatening dream to feel an uncomfortable weight on her body. Blinking into the gray light that was just beginning to filter into the room, she saw a dark head close—within inches of her own.

Her immediate response was to move away, but she was held fast by the heavy arm that was flung carelessly over her breasts. Thad's warm breath stirred the hair around her ears and she pushed at him with her foot.

"Mmmmmm," was the only answer, other than a flickering of a sleepy smile. He didn't awaken, nor did he lift his arm.

"Thad, move over. You're on my side," she whispered, resisting an impulse to brush the hair away from his forehead.

The arm tightened and a leg was thrown across her thighs. "Thad! Wake up!" she whispered sharply. She could feel the heat of his body burning her flesh and she realized that her gown had twisted and crept up during the night.

She was on her back and he was facing her and before she quite realized what was happening, he had rolled her over toward him and her body was held in an embrace that was anything but sleepy.

"Let me go! You promised you'd stay on your side!"

"I did," he murmured into her hair. She could feel a pulse in his throat throbbing against her cheek. "You wouldn't stay on your own side, though, so the rules are suspended."

A quick glance at the ornate mahogany bedstand was enough to confirm her sudden fears. They were both entwined on what had been Thad's side of the bed and from the way he was beginning to nuzzle her throat, he was not about to let her escape scot-free!

"Did you know you're lovely when you wake up, Mrs. Creed?"

She pushed his hands away from her breast and tried to turn her head away. It was no use. He held her with an arm and a leg and when his mouth closed over her own, she knew she didn't want to escape. She felt his fingers at her throat and then her gown was pulled aside, its buttons undone, and his lips followed where his fingers had led the way.

"I want to kiss you all over that lovely body," he muttered hoarsely, "Here . . . and here . . . and here."

Her head twisted on the pillow and a moan escaped her lips as a deep, primitive longing swelled up inside her. Thad opened her lips with his finger and captured her mouth with his own as he moved over her. Against her feeble protests, he whispered soothing love words.

"I know I promised, darling, not too far, too fast, but . . ." She felt him shift slightly and heard the thin sound of snaps giving and then another sound—the strident call of an alarm clock in a nearby room.

"Oh, no!" Thad groaned, collapsing in a way that pushed the breath from her lungs. Her agony was scarcely lessened when he rolled away, turning his back on her.

When her clamoring senses subsided enough, Lyle was dimly conscious of his having left her side. From the hallway, Luke called out softly, Thad answered, and Lyle only hoped the unfamiliar pitch of his voice would be excused due to the early hour.

She couldn't face him, could never bear to look in his mocking eyes again after this. While the shower ran a few feet away, Lyle buried her head in the pillow, her fists tightly clenched beside her. When, after five minutes, she heard Thad emerge again, she pretended to be asleep and was forced to remain in agonizing stillness while he dressed. Her eyes were closed tightly, but not against tears; the utter devastation she felt went far too deep for tears.

She heard the slide of change across the polished surface of the dresser and knew Thad was ready to leave. His footsteps crossed the floor, muffled by the faded floral carpet, and then they paused and returned, to stand beside the bed.

"Lyle—will you be all right?" He sounded so hesitant, so—was it concern? He sounded nothing at all like the mocking, arrogant man who would use her to assuage his own needs, then think nothing of leaving her when he was ready to call a halt to the whole farcial marriage.

"Lyle! Look at me!" He shook her shoulder and defiantly, she rolled over onto her back and glared up at him.

"I'm fine!" she cried in a shrill whisper. "Why shouldn't I be?"

There was a baffled look on his hard-bitten face and before she could escape him, he grabbed her shoulders and hauled her up to a kneeling position on the bed. "Don't do this to me, Lyle," he implored.

"Don't do what to you? I think you're a little mixed up, aren't you? You were the one who was about to—"

"About to what? Don't pull that with me, Lyle! You were going as strong as I was and if it hadn't been for Luke's alarm clock, there would have been no turning back."

"And that would be a shame, wouldn't it? Divorce takes so much longer than a simple annulment! We had a lucky break!"

Her eyes were brimming now and her voice shook perilously and Thad clamped her arms in a crippling grip.

"Oh, Lyle!" He dropped her and turned away, his back hunched as though he were hurting. "Wrong timing, wrong handling. Sometimes I wonder if we'll ever get this mess straightened out!"

Before she could reply, if indeed there had been words to cover such a hopeless situation, Luke called up the stairs. His voice was muffled through the bedroom door but Thad strode across the room without a backward glance.

She was still submerged in fragrant suds that evening when she heard Thad come in. Timing excellent, as usual, she thought wryly, bracing herself to greet him as if nothing had happened.

"I'll be out in five minutes," she called.

"No rush. I'll shower in Luke's bath."

She heard the door close behind him and hurried to get herself dressed before Thad came back. It was only as she stood in front of the dresser in the sleeveless oyster white satin that she saw the disfiguring marks on her arms. Before she could hide her dismay, the door opened and Thad entered, clad in black pants and socks and a ruffled white shirt still opened to the waist to reveal his tanned, muscular chest with its covering of dark hairs.

"Mmm, you look . . ." his voice trailed off. "Oh, no," he breathed, "did I do that?"

"It's all right Thad," she cried, wanting only to wipe out the look of self-loathing from his eyes. "I bruise easily, that's all."

"That's *all!* I manhandle you, almost break your arms and you tell me it's nothing? Lyle, don't you know it kills me to see you marked up like that? And to think I did it!"

"Thad! Stop it!" By some peculiar shift, she was the stronger now, comforting the tall, powerful man who stood so helplessly before her. "Look, I—if I so much as bump into a piece of furniture it leaves me black and blue. It doesn't mean I've been hurt. Just one of the penalties of being a thin-skinned redhead. Now, it's getting late and you're still not dressed. We need to get a move on. Here," she took his tie from the bed where it had fallen, and turned to face him. "Button up and let me do this for you. I'm really quite good at it. Learned it when I was a little girl and I had to stand on a chair to reach my father's tie. That was in the good old days before they struck it rich, when he couldn't afford a dresser." She was amazed to find herself so relaxed with him. You've come a long way baby, as the saying goes. "Now bend over. Mmmmm, you smell nice."

It was almost like playing mother, she thought with a strange feeling of satisfaction. How wonderful it would be to be mother, child, lover and friend to this man she had married. How utterably wonderful if . . . enough of that! She strove to bring her mind back to the task of getting through the evening's festivities. Whatever was between her and Thad must take a backseat until this project was well launched.

"But what about—," he nodded at her bare arms, pain still visible in his eyes.

"Oh, that's easy," she improvised quickly. "The brown lace jacket, remember? It will look just the thing over this oyster satin, wait and see."

She slipped on the coffee-colored, crocheted jacket and, true to her promise, it looked as if it had been designed to enhance the simple, sleeveless dress.

"You look beautiful, did you know that?" he said as they stood ready to go downstairs together. "Your hair—I like that thingamabob you've caught it up with."

She had topped her chignon with an openwork tortoiseshell comb that had been Hesty's, something Pam had insisted she take when they were disposing of personal effects.

"Thank you, Thad. You look rather beautiful, yourself."

He leaned closer and breathed in the fragrance she

had sprayed over her head and shoulders. "I love the smell of your hair," he told her softly, creating a dangerous melting sensation in her center.

"It's not my hair, it's my Degagé," she said, striving for an offhand effect.

"No, it's your hair. I remember the first time I ever felt the vitality of it, on that first night when I thought you were Pam, remember? Even then it smelled like this and I couldn't relate you, with your fuddy-duddy clothes and your prim mannerisms, with such a delicious fragrance."

She felt her pulses flutter as she looked directly into the warmth of his eyes. He was much too close for comfort, and highly dangerous in this disarming mood. She strove for composure as she gathered up her gloves and evening bag. "I expect we'd better hurry. They'll be waiting," she said shakily.

"Promise me something, Lyle—that you won't ever have it cut."

"Oh, Thad, what possible difference—"

"Just promise!"

"Oh, all right, only we have to go now," she conceded breathlessly.

The speakers were brief. Too brief, in the case of her own husband, Lyle decided. Thad proved to be an engaging speaker and she could only marvel at still another facet of this man she had married without even knowing him.

Without knowing him, perhaps, but not without loving him. The fact bore in on her all too forcefully as they danced after the banquet.

The lights were a peach-colored glow and the music

was dreamy as she circled the floor in Thad's arms. She had reason to give thanks to the miserable hours she had spent learning to dance under the grim tutelage of Miss Arva Picler, Pickles, of course, to her twelve- to fifteen-year-old charges.

"What are you thinking?" Thad murmured against her hair.

Lyle stifled a giggle. "One-two, one-two-three, Miss Camden, you're *not* stomping grapes!"

He roared, causing several heads to swivel around. Lyle could not have cared less. She even found it hilarious when, carried away by the pure bliss of the moment, she began to hum along with the orchestra—off-key, as usual—only to have Thad ask if she were ill.

The lights signaled a rest for the musicians and reluctantly, they returned to their table. "You're a delight to dance with, Mrs. Creed, as long as you keep your mouth shut." Thad informed her as he seated her at the secluded table.

"If you're going to insult me, Mr. Creed, I'll have to insist on another glass of champagne. I can't take such painful comments without suitable anesthesia."

There had been perhaps too much wine, altogether, but she was determined to wrap the evening around her and snuggle down in its warmth, reveling in every second against the time when she would be forced to face cold reality. She had found herself arguing with an inner voice at odd times during the day, trying to convince herself that it would be possible to forget Cora, to take what she wanted so badly from Thad and live her whole lifetime in the few weeks—days, possibly, she had left with him.

Thad had turned away to greet a couple who were

waiting arm in arm for the music to start again and he turned now to introduce them to Lyle.

"Charles and Eva Blane, honey. People, this is my wife, Lyle."

Lyle reached across the table to take the hand Charles Blane extended as she smiled at his wife's acknowledgement. There was something elusive about Eva Blane, a resemblance to someone she knew, but it slipped away before she could capture it.

"Charles is project coordinator for the Towers job, Lyle. He's had to put up with me a lot during the past few months."

"No problem, Mrs. Creed. Maybe next time you can . . ." He broke off as a familiar voice cried out from behind him.

"So this is where you all have gotten to! How'd you escape the solid citizenry so soon, Thad, darling? If I'd known you were going to be in here I would have come earlier." Cora completely ignored Lyle as she ran her hand over Thad's arm. He was still standing, for there was no room at their tiny table for the Blanes or for Cora.

As if the earth had suddenly cracked at her feet, Lyle sat in frozen misery and stared down before her, unable to greet the other woman. She could see the bottom of Cora's scarlet chiffon skirt beyond the white tablecloth and as she watched dully, a pair of black shoes joined her.

"Lyle, dear, look who I brought you. Isn't it lucky we happened to run into each other?"

There was no help for it. Lyle knew before she ever raised her face that it would be Stan. Something in the smug satisfaction in Cora's voice had alerted her to the fact that from now on, Cora Lambert held all the aces.

"Hi, Lyle. Good to see you again," Stan greeted her diffidently.

She smiled woodenly as introductions were made and as she watched Thad measure the younger man with a cool, slightly remote look.

Cora turned to Thad, "Did you know I have your little Lyle to thank for this gorgeous hunk of man, darling? Why, if it hadn't been for your bride—but, of course, she wasn't your bride then, was she?" She laughed archly and pulled Thad onto the dance floor with a bright suggestion that Lyle and Stan had a lot of catching up to do.

The Blanes moved off and as Eva smiled over Charles's shoulder, Lyle was struck by the resemblance to Cora. Hadn't Thad mentioned a sister somewhere? It had to be Eva, and Charles, then, was the business associate.

Stan led her unresisting body onto the dance floor, but her thoughts trailed the striking couple who were moving to the music on the other side of the room. Thad in a dinner jacket looked stunning, his rugged features serving only to make the other men in the room look innocuous.

"You look gorgeous. What on earth have you done to yourself?"

"Tactful as ever, aren't you?" The Lyle of four months ago would have been crushed by Stan's clumsy remark. How far she had come!

"I had no idea you were married, Lyle. I must say, it seems to agree with you. How long has it been?"

"Since I married? Oh, not long." She didn't want to talk about her marriage. In fact, she didn't want to talk at all, but a moment later, glimpsing Cora's head resting against Thad's chest, her arm wrapped about his neck in an unnecessary intimacy, something in her stiffened.

"Tell me what you've been up to, Stan, and what you're planning for the future. Any good leads or are you just bird-dogging around hoping for something to drop in your lap?" She beamed up at him, hoping Thad was watching.

The character of the evening changed drastically after that. The lights seemed harsher, the music more discordant and Lyle's head began to ache as she watched Thad and Cora stop to greet people they obviously both knew well. Stan was her only salvation and, as if he sensed something amiss, he stayed close to her side.

It was well past two o'clock when Thad appeared to demand that she dance with him.

"You might ask politely," she asserted, moving reluctantly out onto the floor with him. Her head was really throbbing now.

"You're my wife, or had you conveniently forgotten?"

"I didn't think it made much difference to you," she said tiredly, wishing she had never come to the dance.

"Well, think again! I don't allow my possessions to be passed around lightly. How long have you known Merrill, anyway?"

"Long enough."

The hand on her back pulled her against him sharply, causing her to stumble slightly. "How long? According to Cora, you knew him pretty damned well. Just what did you hope to accomplish by hiding the relationship from me?"

Hating him, hating the traitorous body that tingled to his hard, warm strength even while he was raking her over the coals, she demanded, "Why don't you ask Cora? She seems to have all the answers. At least, all the answers you're interested in!"

"What's the matter, are you jealous?" Gold-struck hazel eyes bore down into her own as if he would read her innermost thoughts and feelings.

Lyle turned her head away, unable to bear his scrutiny. All he could possibly see in her eyes was the agony she was feeling at the moment and it would do her no good to have him know that.

"For your information," Thad gritted through clenched jaws, "Cora lives with her brother-in-law and sister and he's project coordinator for the Towers job. I can't avoid her completely!"

"Why should you?" She smiled too sweetly at him as the music came to an end. "Stan's asked me for the next dance, so if you'll just return me to him, we'll make plans for the rest of the weekend so that you'll be free to spend as much time with your coordinator as you want to."

The hand on her arm tightened until she was certain she'd have a new set of bruises by morning, but Thad was prevented from saying whatever brought the look of baffled fury to his face by the appearance at their side of Luke Simpson.

"We're leaving now, Thad, but you all stay as late as you want."

Lyle saw Stan nearby and practically ran to drag him out onto the floor with her. "Pretend you really like me, Stan," she whispered urgently.

"Pretend! Why honey, I do. What's cooking under that flaming mop of yours, hmmm?"

"Do you like me enough to lend me your car?" she pleaded. A plan was formulating in her head that seemed quite logical to her distraught mind. It took two dances and another drink before she could persuade Stan to leave his car down the street from the Simpson's with the keys under the hood.

Lyle insisted on sleeping on the chaise that night and Thad, thin-lipped and stormy-eyed, did not argue. As soon as he was breathing evenly, Lyle got up and dressed carefully, putting her nightgown and toilet articles into her overnight bag. She did not take the oyster white satin; she never wanted to see it again. As she crept out of the house shortly before dawn, she silently asked the Simpsons' forgiveness. She'd have to write but heaven knows what she could say.

Rolling over the Pasquotank bridge a few minutes later in Stan's Mustang, her mind returned relentlessly to the short, fierce exchange of words between her and Thad on the way home the night before. Thanks to the colorful account Cora had given him of the meeting at Christmas, with Lyle and Stan staying at the same motel and shopping for clothes for Lyle together, any chance of a friendly relationship with Thad for the duration of their marriage was ended. And as for her brief, futile hopes for something more, well that had all been a fantasy on her part, anyway. Never had Thad even pretended to love her—lust was one thing but the stuff of which marriages were made was not a part of their relationship and the sooner they both faced it and ended this farce, the better. She would go away as soon as she collected her things and let Thad know where he could contact her through a lawyer.

There was Thad's house—she dare not think of it as home. It was bad enough to have shown such poor judgment in allowing herself to grow attached to the house, but to have the catastrophic misfortune to fall in love with its owner was going to make the going rough for a long time to come.

It took very little time to pack her things, since she was determined not to take a thing Thad had provided. She raced through the chore without even bothering to turn on the furnace until she suddenly realized she was shaking from both cold and exhaustion. Probably nerves, too, she conceded, rummaging in the kitchen for a bit of cheese to stave off her weakness. She may as well have a hot bath. It certainly wouldn't do to come down with a cold at a time like this!

Between the bedroom and the bath, her restless mind sifted the images of the past twenty-four hours. How could he have believed that witch? It was so blatantly obvious to anyone with their wits about them what Cora was up to! How could he be so blind as to believe the worst? It wasn't as if she, herself, had ever given him any reason to doubt her word—certainly not as much as Cora had.

The more she thought, the angrier she became. She paced back and forth, waiting for the tub to fill, throwing toilet articles into a heap on the chair, lest she forget to pack them. She paused before the mirror and glared at her image.

"What a smart female you turned out to be, Lyle Camden. Lyle Creed. That's a laugh! For Hesty's sake, Lyle . . . you can trust me, Lyle . . . you're beautiful tonight, Lyle . . . that hair. All the gentle words he had said echoed in her mind, but they made scant headway against the tide of furious insults he had hurled at her the night before.

The hair . . . Well, that, for the starters, she could do something about!

Without pausing for thought, she found the scissors

where she had tucked them away with her sewing kit and, loosening the coils around her shoulders, she grabbed up a handful and started whacking.

By the time she left the bedroom for the bath, there was a trail of lingerie across the floor and a glowing heap of hair beside the dresser. She didn't even glance in the mirror as she lowered herself into the steamy tub.

Not until the heat began to leave the water did she stir, swinging her head from side to side in growing amazement. The light-headedness—she had not known that feeling for ages! A good beginning for a new life, and this time there would be no lowering of her defenses. This time, she was not a foolish, inexperienced girl, ripe to fall head over heels in love with the first man to look her way.

She stood up and opened the shower curtain, reaching for the towel. Joyful thought, no more waiting for hours for her hair to dry! Wash and wear, that's what it was! The water gurgling down the drain blotted out all other sounds and it was not until the door was flung open that she knew she was not alone.

Helpless, she stood there like a rabbit impaled on headlights, and stared at a Thad she had never seen before. If she thought she had seen him angry before . . . The towel dropped silently from her nerveless hand.

"What have you—?" he began, glaring in disbelief at her shorn head. Then his eyes dropped to her completely vulnerable body.

Lyle stood frozen. She could not have moved if her life depended on it, and as every vestige of color left her face, she swayed, clutching the shower curtain for support. Dimly, she was aware of a rasping sound, as if the breath were being torn from someone's lungs.

"Oh, my, you little fool, what the hell have you done to yourself?" Thad groaned.

"Darn you," she whispered hoarsely. "Why did you come here?" She yelled at him, oblivious to the water that dripped from her head to join the angry tears that were streaming down her face. "Get out! Get out, I tell you!" She was holding onto the shower curtain in an effort to cover herself and trying to reach her towel on the floor at the same time and all he could do was stand there and stare at her!

"Well, say something!" she cried shrilly past the sobs that tightened her throat. "Is your first and last love with you? Why don't you invite them all in? We'll have a—"

"Shut up, darling." The words were spoken so softly that she was completely shattered. She dropped to her knees on the damp, hard floor and bawled aloud and when she felt gentle hands raising her up, she only cried louder, cried for all the love inside her that was never wanted, for all the hurtful words that seemed to follow her, no matter where she went, what she did.

"I m—must be some s—sort of a—of a Jonah," she wailed as he picked her up, dripping wet and completely bare and pushed open the bathroom door with his foot.

"Heaven knows what you are," he sighed, "but whatever it is, I'm doomed to love it to distraction, so you may as well stop running."

He laid her tenderly on the bed and pulled the cover over her, then he simply stood there and stared down at her.

Lyle was miserably conscious of her cropped hair, of her wet, red eyes and wobbling chin and she glared at the middle button on his black wool flannel shirt. Then, as his words reached her, she gulped, sniffed and raised her eyes to his.

"What did you say?" she whispered shakily.

"You heard me," he growled, lifting the blanket and slipping in beside her. He turned to her and propped his head on his hand. "I've never worked so hard for so little in my life before and I'm telling you, girl, you're through running. You're through hiding behind that shield of yours, ducking away whenever I threaten your precious security. It's time you grew up and started acting like a woman."

"Well, what do you think I've been acting like?" she demanded, sitting up beside him furiously. Only when the cold air struck her did she realize she was naked, and she pulled the blanket up under her chin.

With a laconic motion, Thad pulled it down again. "I'll stoke up the furnace if you're cold, but when I said no more hiding, I meant just that."

She slid back down, all the time staring up into his face as if she had never seen him before. Indeed, she had never seen him in quite this mood and it frightened her—thrilled and scared her at the same time. "What did you say earlier?" she whispered.

"About hiding?"

"No, before that."

"That I love you? Didn't you know?" He tilted his head quizzically and traced the outline of her lips with one finger.

"You didn't love me when you married me," Lyle protested softly, too bemused to argue.

"Oh, yes I did. Maybe not when I announced our engagement but I was already halfway there and by the time I got you under my wing, all signed, sealed and delivered, I knew there'd be no turning back for me."

"But—what about Cora?" She hated to bring up the name, hated any intrusion into the warm, wonderful world she was only now daring to believe in.

"I'm going to tell you this much and then—well, I'll show you," he told her forcefully. His hand was finding its way beneath the blanket to caress her to the point where she found it hard to concentrate on his words. "I was infatuated with Cora, I suppose, and when she dropped me for Bill Lambert, I decided I had had it with women, except for the casual affair. Then you came along and you weren't the material for a casual affair. The problem was, that didn't stop me from wanting you. You're the most aggravating, intriguing, frustrating female—did you know that? Teasing, tantalizing and ducking back behind that wall of yours. Cora simply doesn't register with me. I had to maintain some sort of relationship with her because Charles and I worked so closely together. In fact, I stayed with Charles and Eva as often as not, but when Cora decided to move in on me, I asked the Simpsons for refuge." He grinned and kissed the tip of her nose. "I'm a peaceable fellow, honey, except when I saw you with Merrill." His voice dropped half an octave and Lyle thrilled at the obvious jealousy.

"But Stan didn't mean anything to me," she whispered, her fingers busy with the buttons on his shirt.

Impatiently, he finished unbuttoning it and tossed it off, following with the belt of his flannel slacks and when he lifted an eyebrow at her, she could feel the color flooding her face. She rolled over on her side, facing the wall and heard his low laugh. Within seconds he slipped in beside her and she felt his hard, warm, hair-roughened body close beside her.

"I went after Merrill as soon as I discovered you

were missing and he filled me in on the details of your relationship. I'm afraid he cares for you more than you thought, not that it will do him any good." He turned her toward him now and touched her lips in a feather-light kiss. "No more words now, darling. I've more important things on my mind."

His lips moved to her breast and she was on fire, pressing his head against her as she told him of her love. Her voice was a series of ever-weakening words as he led her from sensation to sensation, and then he was above her, his eyes burning darkly into her own. "I won't hurt you, dearest love. You mean more to me than anything in this world and I'm going to do my best to make you care for me at least half as much." He was punctuating his words with tiny, nibbling kisses and his hands worked a magic over her body until she felt like screaming at the exquisite tension that was building, building, threatening to engulf them both.

Long after she had recovered from her free fall through space, Lyle touched Thad hesitantly on the shoulder. Her face was buried in his chest and his arms had not released her. When she wondered in a timid whisper what the Simpsons thought of her, he smiled enigmatically, his eyes still closed.

"That you're beautiful, but slightly wacky."

"Beautiful!" Aghast, she touched her shorn head. She had forgotten all about that. "Oh, Thad, I must look dreadful! How can you bear to even look at me?"

"Beautiful, my love," he murmured, rubbing his chin over the soft curls that clustered on her head. "As an architect I see far more than surface prettiness, sweet, and right now you look like a Botticelli angel—not that it's an angel I'm wanting in my bed at the moment." His eyes opened lazily and there was no mistaking the look in them as, with an incredible expression of warmth, he rolled her over on her back and grinned at her. "Long after these glowing coals have been covered by gray ashes, I'll still be wanting you, my precious— the way I want you now—again."

His voice deepened and his fingers played on her body with a sensitivity born of knowing. "You'll fill the rest of my life, darling, and if I'm lucky, many more lives after this one. And now, no more talking for awhile, hmmm?"

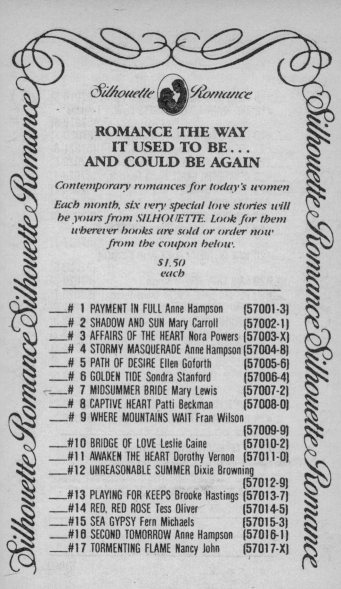

Silhouette Romance

ROMANCE THE WAY
IT USED TO BE...
AND COULD BE AGAIN

Contemporary romances for today's women

*Each month, six very special love stories will
be yours from SILHOUETTE. Look for them
wherever books are sold or order now
from the coupon below.*

*$1.50
each*

SILHOUETTE BOOKS, Department SB/1

1230 Avenue of the Americas, New York, N.Y. 10020

Please send me the books I have checked above. I am enclosing $_____
(please add 50¢ to cover postage and handling for each order, N.Y.S. and N.Y.C.
residents please add appropriate sales tax). Send check or money order—no
cash or C.O.D.s please. Allow up to six weeks for delivery.

NAME_____

ADDRESS_____

CITY_____ STATE/ZIP_____

SB/10/80